2

Dear Oliver,
Hope you enjoy
these tales.
Thanks so
much!
[illegible]

ROBERT FORD

COLLECTED SHORT FICTION

Cover Design by whutta.com

Blurred Images Press

To my fellow dime-store shamans with tales to tell.

We're all completely mad.

You know that, don't you?

ACKNOWLEDGEMENTS

There are many things that shape and form a writer over the course of their life. There's nature and nurture and prods and pushing and a lot of people telling you you're insane. You can't do that. You'll fail. You're wasting your time.

But there are many who encourage and cheerlead. There are those who say the right thing at the right time. Sometimes they know it and sometimes they don't.

Thanks to all of you who ever gave me a nod and smile of "*well done*"... thanks to those of you who gave thoughtful notes on edits and advice on how I might make things better.

But most of all... thanks to those who gave words of discouragement. Moments of pain or doubt.

For that last group... you'll always be *number one* in my book (if you know what I mean). Every time you tell me I'll fail, you provide the fuel for late nights and pushing forward.

TABLE OF CONTENTS

INTRODUCTION

I remember pieces of the puzzle, but my mother tells me when I was in kindergarten, I once led a revolt. Apparently the class was supposed to be drawing pretty pictures of their favorite thing.

I, quietly and off to myself, colored in a large construction paper Superman cape and trimmed it out to shape, punching holes in it and threading it with yarn.

A classmate saw what I was doing and abandoned his project, beginning to create his own cape.

Then another.

Another.

Until a large group of us (almost all of the class, really, except for that blonde girl who liked to eat Elmer's Glue), were all cutting out capes and coloring them in.

I never got in trouble for it. Not really. I mean, it's not as if I stood on a desk with a pair of safety scissors and a box of Crayons, screaming FREEEEDOMMMM!

But it was one of the first times I recall seeing the effect of creative thinking on a group of people.

I've been very lucky to have had some great influences on creativity in my life. Very fortunate to have had English teachers who *got* me and how my mind worked.

I began watching people as a child. Studying their mannerisms and how they spoke. Doing my own sort of profiling, I suppose. I was the gargoyle in the corner, keeping quiet and listening to the adults telling their stories around a card table late at night.

That habit never left me, which is why, I think, my stories tend to have heavy emphasis on the characters. Readers seem to notice, which makes me very happy, and they seem to enjoy the style in which I tell tales, which makes me even happier.

There's a range of tales in this collection, from the bloody and brutal, to the subtle and emotional. They also span a long amount of time of my life. Maybe you can see the development of myself as a person and as a writer, because as the old saying goes, the only thing constant is change.

Be good.
You keep readin' and I'll keep writin'.

Bob

RACING THE MILK

Dear Janie,

It's been a month since you died and I came across your journal today. I guess it's only fitting I pick up where you left off huh?

I'm doing okay, I guess. Tommy told me to take some time off work. At first I argued with him, but I suppose it's best right now because I can't concentrate worth a damn. I've starting watching *Young and the Restless*. Now I see why you made such a fuss about it. I'd tell you Victor's still alive and never died in that car crash, but I guess up there, you already know the plot lines huh? Ha ha.

I miss you honey.

I get angry sometimes even though I know you wouldn't want me to. I think about what our baby would be like. I don't understand why it had to happen like this. Why would God let you get pregnant only to steal you both away from me?

I still remember when you told me you were pregnant. You were, and still are, the most beautiful girl I've ever known. Through everything, you were still beautiful to me. But that morning, you looked so happy. Complete.

I can still picture you smiling. I called in sick and we spent the day in bed together, remember? You would have made an incredible mother, Janie. I know you would have. You always wore your heart on your sleeve and I think kids understood that.

But what's happened has happened and I know I need to stop getting angry. It's not healthy and makes me feeling sick and dead inside.

The apartment is so empty without you. People kept stopping by to bring food and check on me the week after your funeral. I know they all meant well but I was really starting to get sick of ziti and lasagna. Aunt Ruthie baked her god-awful tuna casserole but I ate it anyway because you would have wanted me too.

I guess enough time has passed and people are getting on with their lives again. It's been two weeks since I've heard from anyone. I haven't slept. I lie in bed at night and stare at the ceiling, cradling you rpillow to my face. It still smells like you.

I'd have given anything to take the pain away from you… to make you healthy again. You know that, don't you?

I miss you Janie. So very much.

Dear Janie,

You always said it's the little things that count and honey, I have to say (like so many other things) you were right. I was at the store today and ran into Andy Guillermo. You remember him? He and his wife Lisa were our neighbors when we lived down on Penn Street in that dump we thought was the coolest place in the world. Holes in the damn walls and you covered one up with that painting of the geese you did in college, remember? We were so young then. Goddamn it feels like that was so long ago, but I guess it really wasn't.

Andy heard about what happened and he said he was sorry. I told him it was nice seeing him again and invited him and Lisa over to *our* place for dinner sometime. *Our place.* It came out, just like that, and I caught myself afterward. There's no more *our, we,* or *us,* is there?

Speaking of us, guess what I found today? Our anniversary wine. It's aging a lot better than I thought it would. I drank a glass for each of us, though I suppose, under the circumstances, I could have drank the whole Goddamn bottle.

I found it completely by accident. I was looking on top of the fridge for some batteries and found it up there with your stash can.

Even now, that can makes me laugh. *Janie's Stash, Good to the Last Toke* painted over the Maxwell House logo in your pink nail polish. Right up to the end, you always kept your sense of humor held pinned to your chest like a badge of courage.

Remember the first time we smoked? You'd already thrown up twice by the time I got home with the weed but after a few puffs you were giggling like a child.

There's a lot of roaches left in the can and I've been thinking (I can see you now, rolling your eyes in your *Oh shit, he's thinking* expression).

Honey, I can't live without you.

I looked in the mirror today and didn't recognize my face. I'm old. Exhausted. Baby, I never thought I could hurt this bad. I never thought I'd feel this tired at thirty-seven.

I have a plan and for the first time, I think I'll actually go through with it. I know youv're thinking about the real estate classes I wanted to take and all those get-rich quick schemes I thought were a good idea at the time, but this is different). There's a handful of joints left in your stash can and I think I'm going to smoke one each day until they're gone.

Then I'm coming to see you.

Dear Janie,

It's Thursday, so you got mail from the kids at the cancer ward. Rainbows and sunshine and things they know would make you smile. Lily drew a farmhouse and a barn and some horses drinking from a pond. I guess she remembered you talking about your childhood. She's such a sweet little girl.

Rodrigo drew a bunch of pictures. I guess it's tough for the kids, not having parents to share them with. Our fridge looks like an amateur art gallery exhibit and I know you'd love every one of them.

Everyone wrote to you except for Stevie and there was a message on the machine tonight from Cammie at the hospital that Stevie wasn't doing well. I always liked Cammie. She was the one who fought with the other nurses to get you in with the kids after visiting hours, remember?

They do what they can to keep their minds occupied. I

know Rodrigo still wears that cowboy hat you gave him and I'm sure Tim will be wearing his Mets cap right until the end.

Remember the day you had them all coloring Superman capes? I never told you, but I saw Cammie peek her head in and walk right back out crying. She knew how happy you made them. They loved you. We all did.

But I guess by now you've been caught up on the gossip of the hospital huh? I know Stevie's with you up there. I'm sure you're playing Go Fish and pretend pirates and laughing yourselves silly. Cammie said he went peacefully in his sleep so I guess that's something to be thankful for.

Good night baby.

Dear Janie,

I went to go see the kids today. They all asked about you and I wanted to, but I just couldn't bring myself to tell them the truth. I was scared of how it would affect them. You were their angel. How could I explain to them that an angel could die?

I know spending time with them was important to you, so it's important to me too, and I'm sorry Janie, but I just can't visit them anymore. Seeing their tiny pale faces and bald heads, smooth as polished marble... I can't take it. Whenever I look in their eyes, I see you.

I look at them and I see Death staring back. I don't know. Maybe it's because they're young, but there's no fear in their eyes — only acceptance of the cold, brutal reality. So fragile and brave, it hurts my heart to see them.

They're so different from the adults in the clinic. Being in the clinic was like sitting in a cemetery. Everyone waiting for the chemo drip, full of fear, and faces like linen stretched over kindling. I think it was fear that if they showed boredom, Death itself would arrive to exchange their attitude for their final passing.

But not you huh? Never you. Whatever life threw at you, you always said you accepted it with *a smile on your face and a song in your heart*. And you did, honey, you really did.

I can't go back and see the kids, Janie. I'm not that strong. You were always the rock. I don't know how you kept it together, fighting for your life while Death was at your bedside.

Come to think of it, you kept it together for everything didn't you? I think after we found out you were sick, I only saw you cry once — that day in the kitchen. It was the only time I ever saw you break down. I can't seem to remember to pay the bills anymore, but I can remember your lone breakdown like it was yesterday.

You had your handkerchief on, the pink one with the skulls I got you down on South Street, and when I walked in, you were sitting at the table with a gallon of milk in front of you.

I didn't understand why you were upset, but I remember holding you while you cried. I wanted to take you away from everything. I'd have done anything to make it better.

Honey, I've been thinking about that day a lot. You told me we're all walking around with expiration dates. We're all just racing the milk to see who'll hold out the longest. I guess you never know.

I love you baby.

Dear Janie,

It's been a while and I'm sorry. Lately, I lose track of time so easily. I packed up your clothes yesterday. I took them down to Father Patrick so at least someone else could get use out of them. Everything got packed except for your black dress and your silver high heels. That's what you wore to the Christmas party the year before you got sick. My God, you had heads turning that night. You looked amazing. That's how I try to picture you most of the time, but then, you always looked stunning to me.

I'm having the worst time getting to sleep. The nightmares won't stop. I miss the sound of you breathing next to me. I miss your warmth. It's always cold in the apartment without your light.

Earlier today I was in the living room and I could have sworn I saw Stevie peeking out from behind the bedroom door. I ran to see but of course he wasn't there. My mind is playing tricks on me I guess.

I'd write more but I took some Valium and they're starting to kick in.

I wish you were here, honey. More than anything.

Dear Janie,

I guess there's no shelf life for good weed. This stuff is just as strong as it was when you were alive. It's crazy, I know, but each time I take a drag, I swear I can feel your spirit...taste your breath. In a way, it's kind of like giving you a kiss.

I miss your kisses.

Tommy called and left a message apologizing, but I had no idea for what until I checked the mail. I got laid off today. I guess I should be sort of upset about it, but I'm not. I'll find something, sometime. I know that's what you'd tell me. All it takes is faith right? Faith and fire.

Your mom called today. I really didn't know what to say to her. She didn't make much sense on the phone and I think she might be on medication. I guess she's dealing as best she can. Like all of us.

I'm so tired. I wanted to write down all the things I should've told you when were alive. All the things I should've done but didn't. Things I wish we were able to do now. But I'm so tired right now. I'll write more tomorrow.

Dear Janie,

I don't know what's happening. I think I might be losing my mind. I came back from the grocery store and when I was putting things away, I opened the pantry and Rodrigo was crouched inside, staring at me. His bald head shone in the darkness and his eyes were jet black. He screamed at me and disappeared, just like that.

I know you're up there looking out for me, but I'm scared,

Janie.

I can't bring myself to call and ask about the kids. Lily was the only one who wrote this week. I don't know if Cammie told her what happened, but Lily's letter was only addressed to me.

She wrote a story about snow. She says snowflakes are angel tears falling from heaven, but it's not because they're sad. Lily says when it snows, the angels are happy because someone did a good deed. They still have hope. I don't.

Along with the story, Lily mailed paper snowflakes and a Polaroid of her and Cammie, wrapped in white sheets and wearing foil halos. I know Cammie must've helped her, because they had on angel wings made of paper and cotton balls. Lily's such a sweet kid. She would have made a wonderful daughter to someone.

I guess pretty soon the whole gang will be together with you, huh? I'm sure you'll make them laugh again.

You could always make me laugh.

Dear Janie,

Lately I've been thinking about the day you died.

I watched your soul leave. After all of the pain you went through, it was horrible and wonderful at the same time. I remember holding my hand to your face and neither of us saying a word, not because there wasn't anything left to say, but because we didn't *need* to. You looked so frail, but that sparkle was still in your eyes. You'll *always* be my sparkle.

I remember you smiling at me and for a moment you were the same strawberry-blonde college girl I fell so ridiculously in love with.

Then you relaxed and I saw your eyes lose their shine. You were gone.

Why'd you leave me Janie?

Dear Janie,

They're here. They're *all* here. I think they were looking for you and somehow they found me.

I'm scared and I don't know what to do.

They're angry.

It's early as I write this, or late, depending on which side of night you're looking from.

They won't leave me alone, Janie. I can hear them, but sometimes I see them too. They move around the house like swirls of black mercury. They came looking for you and found me instead. But they're not like they used to be.

I woke up this morning to find our wedding album ripped into shreds on the living room floor. You were torn out of every photo and everything else was in pieces.

I heard Lily laugh in the hallway, but she sounded... mean. When I went to the hallway, *Where is She?* was written in a bright pink scrawl. I've read enough of Lily's letters to recognize her handwriting.

Honey, we didn't even have Crayons in the apartment.

In the bedroom at night, they keep toying with your dress hanging in the closet. I hear them picking through your jewelry.

I tried sleeping on the couch but I can feel their fingers push up through the cushions, poking my spine from beneath.

Rodrigo, at least it sounded like him laughing, scratched the blood out of me yesterday while I was taking a shower.

They whisper to me when I close my eyes...the most *God-awful* things.

I can't stop hearing them whisper.

Happy Valentine's Day, baby.

I know this was never a big day for you. You thought it was a shame that for one day only, people showed how much they cared and loved someone else, but I hope today you'll make an exception.

Remember my plan to come see you? Well, everything seems to be working out. I told you I'd follow through with this until the end. I'm down to the last joint in your stash can, and I guess it's not very surprising it landed me on Valentine's Day.

Honey, I never knew what my purpose was. I never really felt like I was doing what I was supposed to. But then, you knew that.

It took me almost thirty-eight years to find out. I'm supposed to lead your kids back to you.

I'm writing this from our claw foot tub. The water's scalding hot like you used to like it. My skin's almost numb from the heat so I didn't feel anything when I made the cuts. I'm not in any pain.

When someone finds me, I hope they read this so they don't think I was depressed over everything. I want them to understand. I *need* them to understand.

I'm not scared, baby. I'm coming to see you with a smile on my face and a song in my heart.

The kids are all here, gathered around. Watching. Waiting. They're not angry anymore, Janie. They're smiling. I think they know what's happening. I think the angels in Heaven itself know what's happening.

It's starting to snow outside.

THE END

EARLY HARVEST

Dear Penny,

I hope you're doing all right, hon. It's been too long and I could tell you were worried about me in your last letter, though I know you'd never push me to talk until I was good and ready.

I've been thinking about you a lot lately. About how fast time goes by. Hard to believe we've been writing to each other going on twenty years now. Guess we're not little girls at Bible camp anymore.

Do you still go to St. Matthews every Sunday? I haven't been to church in so long I'm afraid I won't remember the hymns, but I believe again, Penny. I have faith. Sometimes God finds you when you need Him the most.

Just the other day, I was thinking about when we hiked back in the pines at Stormy Creek and found that cold spring hidden in the ferns. We swam there all day, not a stitch of clothes on. The sun smiling down on us... splashing and laughing. Seems like so long ago.

It's been a long, long time since I felt that good, Penny. For years I've been one of those canaries my pappy used to take in the coal mines up in Yankstown. Remember how they used to carry them in the mine shafts to see if the air was ok to breathe? For such a long time, I've felt like I was surrounded by darkness, waiting to see if I was living in bad air.

You remember the summer we helped my Granny tend her garden? Eighty-two years old, widowed for ten, and still going strong. A twinkle in her eyes, and still serving the best damn cherry pie around these parts. Granny taught us a lot that summer, but it sure took me a long time to understand. Beautiful flowers all around, but the weeds sneak in if you don't pay attention.

I've been tending my gardens Penny.

I miss you, hon. I wish we could be little girls again. I wish we could start over like seedlings in fresh-tilled dirt and get another chance. Maybe grow in different ways this time around, huh?

I tried so hard to make Henry happy, but I guess I was never enough. You remember my Aunt Ellen? She was the one that used to smoke Pall Mall 100s and hold séances in her field where the Cherokees were supposed to be buried. Ellen used to say that all men are whores and all women are bitches. I guess a little bit of me always knew the first part was true enough, though I didn't really want to believe it.

Not until I found out about Henry and Sheila.

Then…well…

When I was a little girl, I used to listen to Pastor Phil preach about how God is everywhere, in everything from the tallest mountains to the tiniest dragonflies in Gatlin. But he was wrong, Penny. God is vengeance. He's quiet redemption with cold, white eyes that waits in a place without light.

God lives beneath the rows of my garden.

But let me back up a bit, Penny. There's a lot to fill you in on, and I'm really sorry it's been so long.

It was early last year when Henry started down at Pullman's Auto. Dirty work, but hell, Henry grew up fixing every rusty junk heap his daddy brought home. Damn near had a wrench in his hand since he was six, and working on the used cars people drive around here didn't amount to much trouble.

It's been a long time since you've been back to Gatlin, and I know it's hard to believe, but the town's grown. More people move down every year, coming from McCannville or Owen to get away from the city folk. Town's are getting grown up everywhere, I suppose.

Pullman's has gotten a lot busier since Henry started. Doing well enough that Pullman had to hire one of the Gover boys as a mechanic and a girl to help work the phones.

Sheila Koyce was the new girl's name. I saw her once when

I was in Beekman's Drug. Pretty little thing. Thin waist and legs on a tiny build. Full of grace as one of those gray barn spiders we get in late September. Don't know what she did before, but she sure wasn't raised on no farm. Her hair was all done up in red highlights and her eyes... her eyes were just as green and full of life as those young fiddlehead ferns up at Stormy Creek.

I can see why Henry did what he did.

I could write lies to you Penny... same lies I told myself for about a month or so. But I know better, honey. I knew what he was up to. I can't even say she was the first. It was the little things I'd notice, you know? The tiny things in a marriage.

I've written to you long enough, you know how he was. When Henry was of a mind, he could be downright sweet, but more than not, he wasn't.

Mornings came and Henry couldn't wait to get to work... started having late evenings with all kinds of excuses on how Pullman was making him do this or that. He didn't seem to be all that mad about it though.

Do you remember the pearl handled pocketknife my pappy gave me? I never told you but a few years back, I gave it to Henry on his birthday. He thanked me and I think it was one of the few times he really understood how much I loved him, you know? He knew how much that knife meant to me and he took good care of it. But since Sheila came along, he'd leave it behind at the house when he left for work. I think maybe he was afraid he'd lose it wherever he was spending time with her. Like I said, I kept lying to myself for too long, but you can't run from the truth forever.

Sometimes, I'd catch her scent on him. Not perfume. Her natural smell. I have to admit I was jealous—envious, even though I know it's a sin. She smelled young and vibrant, full of life and passion that hadn't been dirtied with tough times.

I'm sure she knew Henry was married. I know she did. But when he was of a mind, Henry could be a silver-tongued devil. He could always get me to do anything he wanted, and I'm sure it was the same with her.

I wanted to hate her, Penny, but I couldn't. I never wanted to hurt her.

Through the end of May I kept thinking about the two of them while I worked in my garden. I put up tomatoes and carrots and cucumbers. Even had a row of beets set in place. I was going to try some cantaloupe, but last year, Lester's goat got loose and ate every damn plant I had. I just didn't have the strength to try them again this year.

Last thing I was getting ready to plant was sweet corn. It was going to be the same kind we used to plant with Granny—the Silver Queen corn that tastes like it was dipped in sugar.

I'd been working the better part of a morning, putting up new barbed wire and turning the soil to get it ready. I was digging up an old root when my hoe thunked hard against something in the dirt.

It wasn't a solid, earthy sound. This was something big and hollow buried in the ground. I knelt down under the May sun and brushed away the dirt to see wide wooden planks set side by side. I used the hoe to keep moving the soil and found more of them. I have to tell you Penny—I got so excited. It was like I was eight years old and finding pirate treasure in the backyard. It was a treasure all right, but this one didn't sparkle and gleam with jewels. It sat dark and full of shadows and swallowed sunlight whole.

I wedged the handle of my shovel under one of the boards and leaned my weight into it, and the end of the board popped free. A cool air washed over me, but the smell, Penny… it was like the swamp water where we used to watch the turtles come out in the evenings.

I looked down in there and it was like staring down a long tunnel. The little bit of sunlight showed rock walls and the water at the bottom swirled with rainbow oil slicks. I stretched out on my belly like a little kid and watched the colors reflecting back. I must have stared down that well for most of the afternoon. I felt at peace and for the first time since finding out about Henry, my heart didn't hurt so much.

Every once in a while I saw the surface of the water break

and the length of eels thicker than my wrist twirl over on themselves. Just as I was getting ready to leave, I saw it Penny.

I saw *Him.*

An arm, skinny and pale as driftwood, stretched from the shadows into the beam of light. I watched as a bony hand turned over and let the sun spill across its palm.

Penny, I know how all of this sounds, but you have to believe me. I don't know how long its been down there. It moved into the sunlight and stared at me. It had large eyes as white as hailstones, flat tapered ears close to its head, and two raw gashes where its nose should be.

It looked at me and smiled... thin slivers of teeth that shimmered in the light.

I know Pastor Phil used to say we could never look upon the face of God. His beauty was so great, we couldn't understand. He was wrong, Penny. That afternoon in my garden, I looked into the eyes of God and I saw salvation.

I sat there and listened for the longest time, hearing whispers sliding over one another inside my head. Then I pulled away and set the boards back in place, covering it all with dirt again. My head was swirling and my heart felt like it was near to beating right out of my chest.

When Henry got home, I had a hot dinner and a cold beer waiting for him. I didn't hardly sleep that night. I stayed awake and thought about what God had told me to do. By the time morning came, it was all set in my mind.

Henry shaved before work that morning. He mumbled something over his coffee about needing to work late, said he had to fix the clutch on Pullman's Cadillac. I just smiled and sent him off to work with a fresh coffee and a bag lunch. After he drove on down the driveway, I noticed he'd left his pocketknife behind. Hell, at that point, I almost expected to see his wedding band sitting beside it.

I sat at the kitchen table and cried for a while, then went out to my garden. It took me a while but I pulled all those boards away and set down a stretch of chicken coop wire across the hole. I spread an old bed sheet across the wire and when I was done spreading dirt over it all, you'd never be able to see what was hidden beneath.

Penny, if anyone can understand, it's you. I just wanted to stop hurting so bad.

That afternoon, close to four o'clock, I got done up in my Sunday best and drove into town and parked about a half block away from Pullman's.

I walked over to Beekman's Drug and used the pay phone outside. Sheila answered in a voice as sweet as honey, and I told her I was broke down with two kids in a car up north of Gatlin on Route 40.

She covered the phone to say something and I heard Pullman yell back to Henry to get the tow truck ready. Henry must've said something back because I heard Pullman tell him he didn't give a damn if he had plans or not.

Sheila told me somebody would be on the way to help me and I could hear the disappointment when she spoke. I recognized it the way I've heard it in my own voice over the years.

I sat in the truck and watched as Henry got the diesel started and drove off. Wasn't much longer when Pullman went off in his Cadillac. No one was left except for Little Miss Hot Pants herself.

You remember when Sadie got sick a while back? She busted from the pasture and got up near Muddy Creek and ate those pin cherries. When the vet came out, he brought horse salts and some other things I had to cut into her feed. He also brought a few syringes of Ketamine in case she wouldn't settle down at night. It quieted her down all right. I damn near thought Sadie was dead in her stall the next morning when I went to check on her.

Sheila was done up in a peach-colored blouse and was busying herself putting on lipstick. I didn't give her time to react. She lifted up her pretty head and I stuck a syringe in the side of her neck, hit the plunger and that was it.

After that ... well Penny, I just don't remember. I guess

God really does work in mysterious ways, because when I came to, I was in the kitchen, finishing up a pot roast and cracking a cold beer for Henry when I saw him pulling into the driveway.

When he walked in the door, he was red faced and serious, looking all kinds of mad. I guess after driving up to Route 40 and not finding anyone that needed towing, he searched for a while and gave up. He gave me an odd look, seeing as I was dressed up pretty, but he didn't say anything. I grabbed my walking stick—you know how my knees ache every time rain's coming along—and I went outside with my evening coffee to let Henry eat in peace.

Henry came out after he was done, carrying a fresh beer with him, and I guess after the day he had, he figured my old farm girl rump was better than nothing at all, because he was all playful when he followed me out to the garden. The sunset was far along by then, and fire shone through the line of maples at the far side of the field.

I almost regretted things then. Henry was making me laugh and we were having such a good time. It felt good, Penny. Like old times, you know? But then I caught a whiff of his cologne and I knew this was just a test from God. Of my will.

We walked on around the bend of the driveway and I saw Henry stop and squint at something moving in the field. A peach-colored stretch of cloth waving in the breeze. I watched Henry's face… the way his head turned a little, trying to figure it out.

I pulled Henry's pocketknife from the hem of my dress and he turned to look down at the open blade in my hands. He glanced back to the field, and I watched his face change when he realized it was Sheila strung up out there in the dirt.

When I stabbed him, I was quick… once, twice, in the center of his stomach, and Henry dropped to his knees. Dark blood seeped from between his fingers and he took a step backward and fell to his knees. He looked up at me and I swung my oak walking stick as hard as I could against the side of his head.

Henry dropped like a sack of feed.

By the time he woke up, I'd bound his hands and feet in bailing wire and dragged him out to the middle of the field. When Henry saw what I'd done to Sheila, he started screaming.

You remember that poison that Granny used to put on her garden sometimes? It was bright pink, the color of fresh bubble gum. I still use it from time to time on my own garden, and I don't know what made me think of it... like I said, Penny, I didn't want to hurt Sheila, and I don't remember doing it, but I filled her mouth with the stuff.

Pink powder was caked along the creases of her neck like make-up. The prettiest shade of color you'd ever want to see. But it did something to her insides, I think. That poison must've made Sheila foam at the mouth because there were gobs of vomit at the edges of her lips. The thing is, between that and her red hair, she was still pretty and that made me even madder.

I stopped messing with Henry and tossed Sheila down into the hole. She tumbled down, quiet as a stone. Sheila didn't grab at anything and when she landed, her head hit first and I saw the end of her dress poof up before she crumpled down into the water. Those eels started thrashing around all at once. I'd be willing to bet none of them have had a decent meal in a very long time.

Henry had been screaming the whole time, begging me to stop, asking me to forgive him. But you know what, Penny? My forgiveness isn't what he should have been asking for. It's not my judgment that matters.

I pulled Henry over to the edge of the well and let him peer inside. I let him stare into the face of Heaven and Henry wept for my redemption, Penny. He tumbled down, bouncing against the rocks and when he landed on his side I heard his ribs break like knots of wood popping in a fire.

I watched for a little while. I saw the eels working at things beneath the water. The whispering was coming back in my head and I didn't want to hear it anymore. One by one I put those boards back in place and the last thing I saw was Henry's eyes flutter open. Then, a bony white hand stretched out from the darkness.

When the last board was set in, I listened to Henry's screams. After a while, he got quiet again and I didn't hear anything but the wet sounds of something eating.

The redemption of the God beneath my garden.

I shoveled dirt all over the boards until I couldn't hear anything, then I went on back inside. Cried myself a little more at the table again. It was too quiet and I couldn't sleep, so I made myself some coffee.

It's late as I write this letter. The wind is blowing something awful, and I know a storm's coming in. The air's warm and the lilacs are out and it smells sweet as cotton candy at the Gatlin fair. I think I'll stand outside until the lightning gets too bad. I want to feel the raindrops on my skin. I wonder if they taste like they did when we were little girls? I wonder if they're still as pure as baby tears and sweet as salvation?

I wonder if they'll wash away my sins?

I don't know what's going to happen, Penny, but I don't feel like a canary in a coal mine anymore. I'm not scared. *I have faith.*

I've been wondering about how my garden will be this summer. Will the corn be as sweet as I remember? Will the tomatoes taste rich and full or will they be bitter? Will there be enough rain to keep them going?

But most of all Penny... most of all, I wonder about what the God beneath my garden will ask of me next, and what will happen if I don't listen.

I miss you hon.
-R

END

BLUEBOTTLE SUMMER

I turned fifteen this summer. The locusts came out a month ago, the crops went to hell and the Kansas City Royals are getting their ass beat. This summer I got my heart broken by a dead girl.

--==•==--

Bluebottle, Iowa is a shitty little smear of a town. It got its name from the first settlers, who for whatever godless reason, decided to stake their claims on the slate-littered ground of this area. None of them had enough livestock to fertilize the fields, so they began adding their own excrement to the soil, creating massive swarms of Bluebottle flies in the process. It is a town *literally* built on shit.

If you drive through town at 55 mph, it'll take less than ten minutes to get from the "Welcome" to the "Thanks for Visiting" signs as you leave. There's four gas stations, two diners, a beauty salon-slash-barber shop, one Methodist church and for entertainment, there's a titty bar called The Foxy Lady. 'Course it's only open Saturday nights, and I've heard the two girls dancing there have about twenty teeth between them. Unless you work at one of those places, there's only a few other options for work. If you want to bust your ass your entire life, die with a farmer's tan and an overdrawn bank account, you could grow corn. If that doesn't suit you, there's the grain mill or working at FireMark making industrial heating parts and breathing in asbestos 'til you can't take a shit in the morning and cough up blood every night.

--==•==--

We moved from Des Moines when I was seven, just after my mother was killed. She grew up here, and was brought here to be buried. To be honest, I think the only reason we moved to Bluebottle was my father's attempt to try to be close to her in whatever way he could. He rarely talked about her at all, except some nights when he got shitfaced on rock and rye.

I still have faded marks on my lower back from his belt buckle, reminding me not to stay around too long when he drank. He'd start swaying slightly, then stop and stare at me accusingly with his glassy, bloodshot eyes. He didn't always get angry. A lot of times, he'd sit in his easy chair and cry to himself, holding his knees and curling up like a lost kid. I'd sit upstairs and wait, listening to him, hoping to hear him say something about Mom. Something I didn't know about her, but he never did. Most often he slurred through his tears about a life without answers, and screamed at God.

I know he didn't mean to yell. He didn't mean to beat me. It was just memories of a bad death. By the next morning, he'd be fine again and we'd be back to having a silent breakfast before he went off to work at the grain mill.

In the time we've been in Bluebottle, my father never brought another woman home, and as far as I know, he never dated. He wore grief on his face like a birthmark, and I think it scared people away.

My dad's brother Frank also lived here. When Mom was still alive, we all used to go camping together for a week each summer. My father would usually drink too much and pass out by the campfire, slumped over in a lawn chair, but Frank and my mother would stay awake long after I was in my sleeping bag.

Frank never married. As brothers, he and my father couldn't have been more different. He always had a piece of licorice or a cold can of pop to give me; a new joke to tell or some funny story. Frank treated me okay, but he was always a little odd in his ways. He seemed as if he was listening to me, but often he would look at me strangely, as if he was studying something in the lines of my face, and I could tell his mind was on other things.

He was a good outdoorsman. Frank taught me things my dad never did. How to wolf whistle through a leaf. How to recognize poison ivy and which berries were okay to eat. I thought Frank was a good man.

--==•==--

It was early June when I found the dead girl. She was lying in the field, hair splayed around her face in a halo of yellow, pure as Iowa corn silk. She wore a simple lavender dress with tiny purple flowers embroidered on the front. It had been ripped away from one shoulder and soaked with blood at the neckline. Her face was a swirling, teal colored mirror and for a moment I thought she was wearing a mask until I stepped closer and most of the flies went away.

She couldn't have been more than thirteen and her throat had been cut from ear to ear.

Her name was Molly Ann, the daughter of Pastor Jack McCullough, and I had heard she'd been missing for several days. They had moved from Boston barely a month ago, and now here she was, dead and lying in an Iowa cornfield while clouds floated by in the eternal blue overhead.

I sat among the rows of corn and watched her, listening to the cornstalks whispering their secrets while the locusts all around us screamed their disapproval.

I don't know why I never told anyone that first day. Anyone else would have told their parents, or called the police. It had been so long since I sat with anyone that would listen, I guess I was just lonely and reluctant to give it up. That night I dreamt of Molly in her lavender dress, alive and laughing and running between the rows of corn. Swarms of Bluebottle flies whirled around her like handfuls of blue-green sparklers and she looked so beautiful and pure and good that I woke up with tears in my eyes, desperately trying to hold onto the dream world where she lived.

The next morning, after my father left for work, I went back to see her, and Molly was still there, undiscovered like a rare artifact. The morning dew strengthened the smell of the pesticide they sprayed over the fields, and the thick, heady odor of abrupt death. I brought a jug of water and a handkerchief and began to clean her up. Her left jaw line was bruised and purple with an angry red stripe of blood running up to her temple. Where the shoulder of her dress had been ripped, mottled blue handprints stood out and a single perlite button held the top of her dress together, holding on by one fragile thread.

I talked to her as I worked. About school and how I couldn't wait to get out. I told her about my father and Frank and about my mother, and how I thought of running away. New York. Chicago. Boston. Any big city would do. Anywhere the land wasn't flat enough to see for miles in any direction.

I washed the dirt from her arms and elbows. Her fingernails had small shreds of skin beneath them and I wiped them away. Her skin looked frosted and sculpted from some kind of pale exotic stone. She was beautiful.

The water in the jug had started to warm from the sun and I soaked the washcloth again, wiping away smears of blood from her face. Her lips were cracked and dry, like field dirt gone too long without water and I ran the cloth over them, giving her what moisture I could. I tried, but I couldn't bring myself to clean her throat. It was crusted but still glistening, like the insides of spring caterpillars. I did what I could, cleaning her up, and wiping away the Bluebottle eggs. There was a single maggot at the corner of her right eye and I folded the washcloth, brushing it away.

And Molly opened her eyes and began talking to me.

She had dark, dead eyes the color of frosted plums and as I sat there and listened, it was easy to drift off in the shadows swirling inside them. I came back to see Molly for the next three days, but it only took that first afternoon to fall in love with her.

She told me about her life. The life of a pastor's daughter and what it was like to grow up in a big city like Boston. She told me of her earliest memories and that she had wanted to be a reporter when she grew up. Her favorite color was purple and she loved horses more than anything else in the world. She told me she wasn't angry with God, but she didn't understand.

And Molly told me what happened.

There had been three of them, she said, all wearing high school letter jackets. They stank of sweat and hard liquor and cigarettes and they started teasing her as she walked home from school. It was nothing but words until one of them pushed her into the cornfield and she had fallen to her knees in the rocky soil; schoolbooks and papers scattered in the dirt.

In the cornfield, she disappeared and they began chasing her, whooping and hollering behind her like jackals. Molly ran until she almost reached the gravel road on the other side of the field, and that's when they pulled her to the ground and held her there. With the three of them, she didn't have a chance.

When she finished telling me, Molly put her head against my chest and cried cold tears, and all I could do was hold her.

She pleaded with me that day to help her. She asked me to kill them. All of them.

--==•==--

Late that night I snuck out of my house. A Royals game was on and I knew my father would be passed out long before the ninth inning had even started. I took his axe from the hall closet and went to the house where Molly had told me to go. All three boys were there just as she said they'd be. And like most homes in Bluebottle, the front door was never locked.

After my axe bit deeply into the first boy's chest, the second boy fell like a sapling willow. By the time I chopped into the last boy's neck, I was sobbing. I could feel Molly slipping away from me even then. All I wanted was to hold her one last time and tell her it was all right. Everything was all right now. But if I went back to the field I knew she'd be gone and we'd never talk again. Her avenged death would bring her rest, but my heart still ached, and I got careless and left the axe behind.

Back in Des Moines, my father had been in the volunteer Fire Department for seven years before we left. The other volunteers had gotten him drunk, given him a party at the fire hall, and handed him an axe with "Firehouse 43" and his name engraved in the bright red blade. When I left it behind, I may as well have signed his name to the killings.

Next morning, the police came into the grain mill just after coffee break and arrested my father in front of everyone. He fought them at first, until they threw him down, cuffed him and dragged him away screaming. I wonder if he looked like he did after Mom died. If he had that same lost, confused expression, full of endless questions with no answers in sight.

Frank came over just after the police left, his face grave and sickly. He told me what happened, then tried to give me an awkward hug, but I twisted away and ran.

My father never claimed innocence, but I think that first night in jail he figured it out for himself. Wasn't too hard really. I mean, hell, there were only two of us in the house with the axe.

The official statement the next day was that my father broke a piece of the metal bed frame in his holding cell and slashed his own wrists.

I'd like to think he did what he did because he loved me. That my father's last act was to try and protect me by taking blame for my actions. I'd like to think it, but it's just not true. I think he was just tired of living with so many unanswered questions.

--==•==--

It only took three weeks of people finger pointing and

whispering at us before Frank asked me if I'd move to Cedar Rapids with him. In a town the size of Bluebottle, murders don't happen often, and when three high school lettermen nearly get decapitated, the townspeople grab onto it like a terrier with a meat bone, and they don't let go easily. I guess Frank figured it was time for a fresh start somewhere else and I couldn't have agreed more.

We talked one night about what happened to my mother. Frank told me some things I already knew, and others that I didn't. He said my parents fought a lot when I was a baby; normal stuff about money and bills, but mostly about my father's drinking.

I don't remember it, but Frank said my father hit her sometimes. My memories of her death are sketchy at best. Seeing her lying on the cheap yellow tile of the kitchen, eyes wide and staring at nothing and everything all at once. Policemen all through the house. Loud squelch of their walkie talkies. My father, just home from work and still in his coat, red faced and trembling, running his hands through his hair over and over as he tried to answer their questions.

In the years since, there had been nothing new on her death. No dramatic breakthroughs or promising leads. My mother was just another unanswered question stuck in a case file somewhere.

Frank gave me that odd, puzzled stare for a moment before wiping his eyes and leaving the room. He came back with two dishes of ice cream and we spent the rest of the night in silence.

I used to go a lot when I was younger, but I hadn't been to my mother's grave in over a year. If Frank and I were leaving Bluebottle, I thought the proper thing to do was to visit her again before we left, but of all the times before, I don't know why it was that last visit when my mother chose to talk to me. To be honest, I think it was Molly that started it. She undid some tethered restraint inside me that changed things forever.

There were some coffee colored flowers at her grave, long

since dried up and bleached of color by the sun. I sat and ran my fingers over the chiseled letters in her granite headstone and as I watched, my mother rose up to greet me.

Her eyes were black-green pits, the scaly, gray skin on her face riddled with holes and pockmarked from insects and time. She wore a simple ivory broach at her neck, and a black evening gown that caught on her thin collarbones. Her dark hair draped in ringlets to frame her face, and her scalp had a slight lilt to it like an ill-fitting toupee.

When she began talking, her words came out in dusty, croaking whispers, and I had to lean closer to understand. I sat there the rest of the day, listening to her speak. Listening to her ask for an avenged death.

It hadn't mattered to Frank that she was married; that it was his own brother he was betraying. Frank had fallen in love with her and for a time, she with him. Mother told me about their affair. The letters, hushed phone calls, and sneaking around. And getting pregnant with me. Frank's endless pleading to run away, and her constant refusal even though his love was turning to a black, bitter anger.

Mother told me everything I didn't know and when I turned to leave her bones chittered like bamboo wind chimes as she eased back into her restless grave.

I was careless with my first axe, but I bought a new one. I like the way it feels when it's in my hands. Thick tempered steel. Familiar smell of lacquered hickory. I like the way it makes me feel when I hold it. And the feeling I got when I killed the boys... well, when I brought it down on Frank's skull, the feeling was just as strong as before.

One thing I didn't realize; once the dead start talking, they don't shut up.

Frank has been prattling on non-stop for the past two days since I killed him.

I've been spending a lot of time out on the front porch

with the doors shut tightly behind me. Yesterday I chopped Frank up and put him in the basement freezer, but I can still hear his muffled pleas, shrieking at me over and over to kill myself.

I wonder how long it'll take someone to wonder why Frank hasn't shown up for work. How long before the cops come out and I'm hauled away? How long will Frank keep begging for an avenged death after I'm gone?

Outside I sit. It's hot, with that tight, sticky, holding-your-breath feeling just before a storm is about to hit, but at least there's a little breeze.

Outside I sit and think of my mother. I think of Molly. I hope they're both all right. At peace.

Outside I sit and try to ignore the wet, screaming demands of Frank to kill myself.

And all around me, the locusts keep screaming.

END

THE TASTE OF OUR INDISCRETIONS

It took Joseph Haslan a full forty seconds before his impatience got the best of him. It was a new personal record.

He studied the crowd in the waiting room. A mishmash of twenty-or-so people sat in orange plastic chairs. Haslan shifted uncomfortably in his own seat.

A brunette woman sat by herself at one of the end row of chairs. Good posture. Legs crossed. Skirt a bit short for this time of year. She reminded Haslan of his late wife, Lori. Attractive. Elegant. Nice taste in clothing. A trophy wife if there ever was one, Lori had lacked something intangible but was so perfectly complete in other ways. She had been happy to receive pearls and diamonds at Christmas and completely content to overlook his side projects of other women.

Well, thought Haslan, *not completely content. She did end up in a Malibu hotel with an empty bottle of vodka and handful of Valium. Checking out of a five-star hotel in a body bag wasn't exactly the classiest move she could have made. People make choices, good or bad. Some choices are just a whole lot shittier than others. Ah well. She knew what she had signed up for when we started dating.*

Haslan surveyed the room. It was long and wide with pure white walls, unadorned with the standard bottom-shelf artwork. The room was empty of brochure stands or even coffee tables piled with outdated celebrity-gossip magazines. The equally unremarkable floor was a gleaming waxed tile.

An enormous cherry-wood desk stacked with manila folders anchored the middle of the room. Haslan pegged the man at the desk to be in his late fifties. Thin build. Wiry. Badly receding short-cropped gray hair. Thick, half-lens glasses rested across the bridge of his nose. He had the appearance of a second-rate Woody Allen impersonator. He had shadowed, tired eyes, with bags bulging beneath them and a nervous, almost self-conscious habit of glancing up at the crowd before turning back to the computer screen on the desk.

A skinny rail of a girl stood in front of Woody as he worked. She wore faded jeans and a gray sleeveless blouse. Greasy blonde hair was pulled away from her face in a loose ponytail. Her arms were crossed in defiance, even though Woody spoke in soft tones. Haslan strained to hear but couldn't make out what he was saying.

The girl let one arm fall to her side and Haslan saw the pucker-mark trail along her forearm. A junkie. She scratched absently at the skin there and nodded at something Woody said, gave an "aw shucks" shrug of her shoulders, and nodded again.

Woody stared at the blue glow of the monitor and typed rapid-fire on his keyboard. He peered through his glasses, mumbled something under his breath, clicked his mouse, and typed again. He repeated the process of studying the monitor, shook his head, and slapped the side of the display.

Haslan snickered at Woody's frustration and checked his Rolex. 11:23. Christ he was late. There was a board meeting at noon and he knew damn well they were armed for bear this time. They'd be asking questions. Hard ones. Trying to ferret out answers he couldn't—*no, wouldn't*—provide. Questions regarding company funds. Retirement accounts. IRA accounts. 401ks. Hopes. Dreams. College educations for entire generations that he had never met and didn't care to.

Fuck 'em. Not my problem. They're all strangers to me. Common working-class vermin who should've known better. Welcome to big business. The American Dream? It doesn't exist at that rung of the ladder.

But, Haslan thought, *it damn sure does for me.*

The Board can ask all the questions they want. By next week I'll be in the Bahamas sipping tall drinks with paper umbrellas and my biggest worries will be what I'm going to have for room service and which island girl I'm going to bang that night. I saw my piece of the pie and I not only took it, I carved the Goddamn thing to pieces.

He felt eyes on him and caught Woody Allen peering over his glasses with a look of disgust.

Another man stood on the side of Woody's desk, an enormous man dressed in simple hospital greens. He glanced at Haslan and turned away. He wasn't just black, but jet, the color of burned cinders, and his bald head glistened under the lights as if it were oiled. He towered over the junkie as he lightly touched her elbow and led her away. She shuffled as she walked and stared at the floor. *Probably jonesing for her next fix.*

Haslan turned away to check a paper ticket stub in his hand: 74301. He looked around the room for a digital ticket sign. Some symbol of progress. Efficiency.

Nothing.

He sighed and crossed his legs, checking the shine on his Berluti shoes. A dull streak stood out along the left side of one loafer.

Goddamn shine boy. These shoes cost more than he makes in four months. The little Mexican bastard, probably right off the boat, had given him the shine that morning. *No one takes pride in their work anymore. No one cares about other people's property. So much for a tip next time, you little prick.*

Haslan felt Woody staring again, ignored him, and checked his ticket once more. The number was still the same. He sighed, feeling his impatience bubble inside him like heartburn.

He looked around at the other people in the waiting room. They stared at the ceiling or zoned out, absently staring at the floor in front of them.

A young mother sat in one corner off to herself, cradling an infant that was surprisingly quiet. She cooed to the baby and raised a hand to tuck her hair behind her ear. In that moment, she reminded Haslan of his daughter, Emily.

It had been years since they'd spoken. Private schools

and summer camps and college tuition and what did she do? Got hooked on coke. A hundred and eighty thousand dollars worth of private rehabs later and Emily had gone on the run.

She'd called him a year later, almost to the day. Sobbed on the phone, apologized, and told him how sorry she was. Asked for help to straighten her life out once and for all.

Sorry Em. The window for help has closed. Be responsible for your own choices.

Except for her crying, she'd gone silent on the phone and quietly hung up. Last he'd heard she was doing porn somewhere in Los Angeles.

The mother smiled at the baby and Haslan heard the tiniest gurgle of happiness in response. There was a smear of red on the yellow blanket swaddling the infant. It caught Haslan's eye and made him wonder about the source.

It also made him think about the women he'd had affairs with over the years. There'd been many. Two stood out, though he couldn't remember their last names.

Both had gotten pregnant and he'd paid to take care of the problems, as well as to keep things quiet. *Another child in my life? No thanks. Especially not to a kept mistress in a Manhattan apartment.*

After the abortions, they'd outlived their use and Haslan had made short work of them. They'd known better from the beginning. They had been nothing more than business arrangements. If they'd thought anything else, they'd been kidding themselves. They could no longer handle the arrangement so he'd discarded them like employees unable to perform their duties.

The light flickered in the room and he turned toward the ceiling. The crowd exchanged brief glances before returning to their blank stares.

An uncomfortable shiver ran through Haslan's body. He shook his head, trying to force it away. Slowly, like sunlight breaking through heavy morning fog, a realization began to form in his mind. A realization Haslan had no choice but to accept: he had absolutely no idea what he was actually waiting for or how the hell he'd gotten here in the first place.

He did a brief mental run-through of his day.

His day had started the same as every morning had for the last fifteen years, since Lori had killed herself.

5:00 alarm.

Grab an espresso to prime the pump and hit the gym for thirty minutes of cardio.

Shower and out the door by 6:15 sharp to stand in front of the Warington Building by 6:25 and read the morning edition of the *Journal.*

He had waited for the shine boy to do his half-assed job this morning and thought about responses to the Board's inevitable questions, smiling as he considered interest-bearing accounts in warmer climates.

When the shine boy had finished with him, already turning his attention to the next man in line, Haslan had noticed the man's off-the-rack suit had a stain along the cuff of his right sleeve.

Slovenly. Unacceptable. Impression is everything.

Haslan had folded his journal, wondering how the Nikkei would turn out later, and tossed a dollar in the shine boy's tip box. He headed in the direction of the Korean fruit stand on 12th and Walnut and then...

Nothing.

Your mind's slipping, Haslan. Pull your shit together. Find some bread crumbs as to how you got here. But first thing's first. It is high time to cut and run.

Haslan stood and let his ticket stub flutter to the floor. He straightened and fastened the buttons on the front of his Fioravanti suit.

He caught Woody's gaze and saw the man's expression of outright disdain. Haslan sent it right back to Woody in spades.

Screw you and your community-college authority, you pompous little prick. I have neither the patience nor the inclination to give you the time of day, let alone wait here in this goddamn—

"Sit down, Mr. Haslan." Woody's soft voice was nasal and thin, matching the frail build of his body, but there was an edge to his tone. The sound of a tired, hen-pecked husband on the verge of losing his temper and backhanding his wife in the middle of a public argument.

Haslan ran through his mental catalog again, finding no recollection of actually speaking with Woody or giving his name. He ignored Woody's request and turned past the row of chairs to his right, searching for an exit.

"Mr. Haslan?"

He kept walking but in his peripheral vision Haslan saw Woody stand up behind his desk.

"Mr. Haslan?"

The quiet murmuring in the waiting room stopped. Haslan felt everyone watching him. Screw them all. He had places to be.

"I said, SIT DOWN!" Woody's voice reverberated through the waiting room like thunder.

Haslan slowly turned to face Woody. The delicate man stared at him, leaning forward over his desk. Soft halos of pure white light glowed from Woody's eyes and his expression showed this was no longer a request. It was a command.

Looking into Woody's eyes, Haslan froze where he stood. He felt tremors of terror wash over him. It had been almost forty years since Haslan had felt honest-to-God fear. Since he'd run from his drunk father, who clutched a leather belt in his fist. But this puny scarecrow of a man in front of him was something else entirely.

Haslan glanced around again for an exit door. However the hell he'd arrived here no longer mattered. What was important was that it was time to leave. He had to get out of here. Now.

Except...

He searched from one corner of the expansive room to the next. There was no exit to be found. There were no doors at all.

Woody stared at him from behind the desk. The light

streaming from the sockets of his eyes flickered like candlelight and Haslan noticed the man's expression had changed. He was peering at him from over his glasses. Grinning.

Haslan's insides turned to liquid. His bladder threatened to give way. A cold sweat trickled down the small of his back and his heart thumped rapidly in his chest.

No, Haslan thought, *I was wrong. This isn't fear. This is something entirely new.* His knees buckled and he slumped into the empty chair behind him. *What the hell is going on?*

"Not exactly, Mr. Haslan." Woody grinned at him a moment longer. The light bursting from around his eyes dulled. He sat down and turned back to his computer screen.

Everyone in the waiting room stared at Haslan. He fidgeted with the cuffs of his suit jacket. Checked his watch again. Still 11:23.

There had to be a way to get out of here. He'd watched the junkie girl get led away to...*somewhere*. But he hadn't actually seen her leave. He looked around the room. Checked behind him.

Nothing.

A flood of panic threatened to rise inside him and he choked it back down. *You're dreaming, old man. This isn't real. Just stress getting to you. Just a little longer now. A week at the most and this will all be a memory.*

Pull.

Your shit.

Together.

Haslan's mouth was dry. More sweat ran down his spine. He loosened his tie and focused on breathing. Slowly. Deeply.

"74301."

Haslan looked up. Woody motioned him forward with a come-hither finger. He tried to stand and for a moment his legs wouldn't respond. He took a deep breath and forced himself to rise from the chair and walk to the desk. To Woody.

Woody pulled a manila folder thick with paperwork and opened it in front of him. He reviewed the top sheet and shook his head as he turned and keyed in something on his computer.

"Your disincorporation case, Mr. Haslan, is...unusual."

"I don't understand..." Haslan glanced around the room once more, hoping an exit had magically appeared since his last search. "I'm not exactly sure what this is in reference to."

"It's been some time since someone of your caliber has been sent here for processing." Woody flipped through several of the sheets in the folder and laughed, shaking his head again. "Usually they're simply re-routed, but management seems to know what it's doing." He cocked his head and rolled his eyes in a gesture suggesting a lack of confidence in his own words, then lowered his voice. "Most of the time."

Haslan searched the man's desk but it was void of a nameplate. A business card. Anything revealing his name. Or the company he worked for.

"Sir, I don't know what all this is about. My... disincorporation?" Haslan leaned closer, speaking quietly. "Are you working with the Board? We can come to an agreement, you know? You'll never have to come to this shitty place to work again. Ever."

Shadows passed over Woody's face and he gave that incredulous chuckle again. A condescending laugh that someone would give to a toddler who was acting out.

"Mr. Haslan...this isn't about money. It's not about the funds you've been hiding. The countless scores of people you were planning on wiping out for your own greed. The college funds you'd planned to steal. The pensions and retirement funds you were funneling into your private accounts." He rifled through more paperwork.

"It's not about the extra-marital affairs or terminated pregnancies from those affairs, which you had insisted upon. Nor how you conveniently ignored the pleas of help from your daughter, packed your mother off to the cheapest nursing home you could find, and successfully plunged a knife into the backs of countless friends and associates in your greedy pursuit of self-preservation."

Haslan's stomach turned. *Oh they were good. Who the hell*

was onto him? How much money would it take to keep his ass out of prison?

Woody closed the folder and let out a long sigh. He folded his hands and rested them on top of the paperwork.

"This isn't about you buying your way out of this. Because you can't. You're dead, Mr. Haslan. Here, we deal in currencies other than money."

Haslan's fear was swallowed as anger pooled inside him. It rose in huge red pulses of adrenaline through his body. His hands balled into fists.

"Are you threatening me, you little twig bastard? You think you know people? I know people too. Lowlifes that would gladly peel back the skin from-"

Woody's eyes flared with white halos again. He leaned forward and grinned wider this time, baring teeth yellowed with age.

Haslan's stomach tied itself into knots and he tasted bile at the back of his throat. He shrank away.

Woody swiveled the monitor around to Haslan and a video clip started to play.

It was footage of him that morning with the shoe shine boy. He stood and tossed a bill into the tip bucket, folded his paper, and started walking. Looked up 15th street and stepped from the curb, right into the path of the passenger bus.

The Wall Street Journal flew into the air, pages fluttering like a covey of doves. Haslan watched the bus slam into his body; his left leg wedged beneath the front bumper and dragged him beneath the front wheel. The forward motion of the bus pulled him lower, forcing him against the concrete curb. The driver's face was horrified, his mouth stretched in a gaping "O" as he slammed on the brakes.

The chrome bumper pressed against Haslan's pelvis, snapping it in two and creating enough internal pressure to make several of his ribs pop through his suit jacket. His leg snapped at an angle against the curb, the femur punching through his thigh in a ragged break as the tire rode against it. Blood sprayed in arcs across the sidewalk.

Air brakes hissed and the tire ground against Haslan's chest, forcing his internal organs out through the ripped flesh his ribs had already punctured.

The tire came to a stop against the underside of Haslan's chin, slamming his head up and out toward the curb. The top of his skull split, the weight of the bus forcing his brains out through the crevice like someone squeezing toothpaste from an almost empty tube.

Bile rose in his mouth and Haslan fought the urge to vomit. The thought came to him that the video was doctored. *Hell, they brought dinosaurs to life on screen years ago. Surely they could've...*

But no. The truth was, he *knew* better. It was coming back to him in bits and pieces. He remembered the driftwood-brittle snap of his own ribs and the burlap cloth sound they made as they tore through his flesh and suit. He could recall the hot-liquid burst as his liver and intestines tumbled out of his body. Feel the cool city breeze against them, exposed to air for the first time.

Haslan turned to Woody. His mouth was bone dry. He closed it again, uncertain of what he wanted to ask. Instead, he checked his suit. No blood. Crisp. Clean as the day it had been tailored.

Woody still had a smile on his face, but its strength had dulled.

"You're dead, Mr. Haslan. But as I mentioned...I'm not entirely sure why you're here." Woody lowered his voice to a whisper. "I've seen some pretty big assholes in my day, but you take the cake."

Haslan worked his tongue in his mouth to create some saliva.

"In my life it was dog-eat-dog, baby. I fought my way to survive and this is where I end up? Here?"

Woody reached up and took off his glasses, laid them on his desk, and rubbed his eyes.

"You're not the typical candidate, Mr. Haslan. You aren't

suitable to process immediately, yet your paperwork…"

Woody put his glasses back on and scanned over some paperwork. "You, Mr. Haslan…are a gray area in our system. Quite honestly, you should probably be swimming in a vat of frying grease right now or...breathing in scent of fresh brimstone. But like I said, the BGIC has a great sense of humor."

Haslan closed his eyes. "I don't understand. The...The BGIC?"

"Big Guy In Charge." Woody leaned forward on the desk and steepled his hands. "I'll admit there have been recent moments where we're all concerned about His...state of mind. We fear He may have become...infirm." He toyed with a stapler on his desk, moving it closer to the monitor as he spoke. "There may be decisions for us to make in the future, but for now..."

Woody stared off in thought for a moment, and then snapped out of his reverie, focusing on Haslan once more. "For now, the choice has been made. You're here and that's what counts. You have reparations to make, Mr. Haslan."

"This...is Heaven?"

Woody tilted his head back and forth, pooching his lip out in thought.

"In the realm of Heaven there are many hells, Mr. Haslan. You stand at the way station of them all."

Haslan's knees went weak. The room alternated from being too bright to having dark phantoms swimming through the air.

Woody gave that grin again.

"Your case assessment is over, Mr. Haslan. Michael will assist you from here."

The same towering black man he'd seen earlier stepped closer and Haslan felt like a child in his presence. Small and afraid of the monster lurking in the shadows beneath his bed.

Strong hands, cool and heavy, pressed against the back of Haslan's neck and he stepped forward. Numb. Free falling.

Trembling inside. His bladder gave way and flooded his legs with warmth. He no longer cared, just kept walking toward a sheer wall of nothingness.

A whisper of cold air. Sunburst flares of blinding white and the waiting room was gone, replaced by a single hallway perforated with red doors spaced every ten feet. The hall extended as far as Haslan could see. Thousands of doors stretching on in the distance until they faded from sight.

Haslan kept walking until Michael stopped in front of a door and withdrew a large key ring. He fitted the heavy brass key into the lock and pushed the door open wide.

There was a shuffling sound in the hall and Haslan turned. A little boy stood, watching them. He wore jean overalls and bright red canvas sneakers. His brown hair was unruly and wild and he gave a lopsided smile full of mischief.

He waved a child's wave, palm up, folding his hand in half.

Haslan gave him the finger.

Michael shook his head.

The boy giggled, turned away, and skipped down the hall.

"Was that..."

"Yep. BGIC." Michael sighed and turned the knob of the door, swinging it wide open. "We're really going to have to make some tough calls around here soon."

Haslan looked through the doorway and saw nothing but darkness. He took a deep breath and stepped inside.

He heard Michael flip a switch and a single light bulb turned on overhead. The room was a vast warehouse with twenty-foot ceilings. Unlike the waiting room, the warehouse was filthy and cold. Grit shifted beneath his shoes on the cement floors.

The room was also filled. Rows upon rows of tall shelves stretched off into shadows. Each shelf was crammed with gallon jugs. Haslan stepped closer. The jugs were crusted at the caps. Stains ran down the plastic sides and collected in pools at their bases.

Haslan stared, confused, and turned to Michael.

"I suggest you take off your suit, Mr. Haslan." Michael jingled the key ring in his hand.

"What? Why?"

Michael walked to the closest shelf and withdrew a jug.

"You need to make reparations, sir. *Every last drop is yours to drink.* I'd hate to see you sucking sin from a four thousand dollar suit. I let you into this room. Only you can open the door from inside. After you've finished."

Michael shook the jug. The liquid inside swirled in a mustard-colored soup.

"This is your life's work, Mr. Haslan. All you've achieved. Every last teardrop and ounce of heartache. Now you get to live and experience it yourself. We reap what we sow, Mr. Haslan."

Michael set the jug on the floor and walked out, closing the door behind him. The lock turned with a heavy metallic clank.

Haslan looked at the single bulb shining above him. He screamed at the shadows. He ran between the rows of shelving until his lungs burned and his chest hammered. Tears streamed down his face. He collapsed to his knees and trembled. Screamed again, loud and long.

There was no echo. The sound was swallowed by the darkness.

His life flashed through his mind. Lori. Emily. His mother. The company. The money. The pain he'd caused. The endless grief.

Haslan took off his suit jacket and let it fall to the floor. He unbuttoned his shirt and kicked off his shoes. Stepped free of his pants and left them in a crumpled heap. Stripped down to his bare flesh.

It was cold in here. He shivered in the darkness.

He turned and held his first jug.

Haslan sat down, cross-legged. The cement floor was cold against his bare ass. He twisted the corroded lid off the jug and tossed the cap into the shadows. He breathed in the scent of the contents. It smelled like sin.

Haslan closed his eyes. Opened them again. Stared up at the light bulb until it burned his retinas and he saw spots dancing around the warehouse wherever he looked.

Haslan tilted the jug to his lips.

Drinking his past.

Earning his future.

And seeking his salvation.

END

FOR GOODNESS SAKE

Marky's breath slowed and deepened into an easy rhythm. He snuggled a tan velvet teddy bear close to his side. Scott peeked at his brother to make sure he was asleep and slowly sat up.

The Buzz Lightyear alarm clock on his bed table hummed 10:18 in neon green. A hardback of *Good night Moon* sat at an angle on the night stand.

There was a waxing moon outside, and low light filled the bedroom. A glow-in-the-dark velvet poster of a king cobra decorated a closet door. The Incredible Hulk stretched his bulging arms from a hanging shoe rack on the closet door.

Scott reached beneath his bed and withdrew what he had stashed there earlier in the day. His hobby of building model planes had come in handy. The rest of the plan had just been creative thinking on his part.

Mark slept so peacefully, good little boy that he was. Smart. Funny. A good listener. Followed *all* the rules. Did a good deed every day.

Scott's stomach roiled. His brother made him sick, but it also made him angry because it was Christmas Eve and that meant Santa was bringing presents.

It meant *Goody-Two-Shoes* would get more.

He turned to look at the milk and cookies they had left on his dresser. It had been Marky's idea to put apple slices for the reindeer.

Fucking *Golden* Boy, Scott thought. The curse word felt forbidden to him, but grown up. Being *bad* felt *good*.

Marky was good all the time and Santa saw it.

That's what Mom and Dad said – Santa sees *everything*. He knows. He's always watching.

Always.

He sees you when you're sleeping.

He knows when you're awake.

He knows when you've been bad or good,

So be good for goodness sake.

If that was true, it meant Santa had seen everything. *Absolutely everything.*

What he had done to the Dearborne's cat. The toads he had found last August and spent an entire afternoon with a magnifying glass and a bottle of bleach swiped from under the kitchen sink.

Scott bit back a laugh. Oh, *that* had been fun. How their skin had sizzled!

He looked at Marky and Scott felt a sudden rush of heat course through his body. He uncapped a tube of model glue and squeezed glistening figure eights on a sheet of plastic wrap.

He slid his hand beneath the plastic wrap and lifted the square, promptly cupping it over Marky's nose and mouth.

Marky struggled fitfully in his sleep. He slapped at his face. His fingers hooked into rigid claws, growing frantic, raking against the plastic sealed over his partially opened mouth. The plastic sucked inward as he attempted to draw breath. Scott held it tightly in place.

Marky's arms went limp. His eyelids fluttered like night moths cupped in eager hands. His whole body relaxed and he lay still.

Scott grinned. He looked through the window at the sliver of glowing moon. He scanned the sky for any streaks that might be a sleigh drawn by flying reindeer.

Did you see *that*, fat man? Did the fuckin elves write *that* on the naughty list?

Too late to return Marky's gifts, but don't worry, I'll just scratch his name out and write mine in.

Footsteps sounded from the hallway and Scott pulled the blankets up to Marky's eyes. He threw the tube of model glue under his bed and jumped under his own bed covers.

The door knob turned ever so slightly. The whisper of

wood as it the door opened. A thin beam of light shone into the bedroom.

Scott closed his eyes and breathed slowly and deeply so his chest would visibly expand and contract. He felt someone watching him.

Low murmurs from the hall and then footsteps walking away.

Scott eased himself out of bed and crept to his door. He angled himself to see his mother standing at the edge of the living room at the end of the hallway. She smiled at something and tilted her head, laughing. Scott could see the reflection of the Christmas tree lights winking in her eyes.

In Scott's line of sight, a man's hand stretched out in a furred red sleeve, trimmed in white.

More of the form came into view, the bulk of a man's back dressed all in red. The figure leaned closer to Mom. Scott heard the wet sound of kissing, more low murmured words, and Mom laughed out loud again.

Scott felt the air rush out of his lungs.

You *Fat Bastard*! You're here early.

His mother raised her hand and Scott saw her look at something sparkling like tinsel on her ring finger. She smiled again and daubed at her eyes.

I saw Mommy kissing Santa Claus.

Underneath the Mistletoe last night.

Scott felt sick to his stomach. His eyes brimmed with tears and for the first time in his young life, he felt the first tickling of betrayal and rage.

Scott ran from the door to his closet. He reached inside one of his snow boots and withdrew a knife he'd taken from his father's fishing box. The blade was long and thin and tapered to a glistening curl at the end.

He stopped at the saucer of treats they had left out, and turned it, ever so slightly, so it would look most appealing, then jumped beneath his covers again, facing toward the cookies. Scott closed his eyes and waited.

Ten minutes went by before Scott heard footsteps in the

hall and the bedroom door creak open. He could feel someone watching him again. He made his eyes flit back and forth slowly beneath their lids, a tell-tale sign of dreaming, or so he had read. He kept his breathing soft and slow. Beneath the covers, he gripped the handle of the fishing knife with a sweaty hand.

The gentle footsteps moved into the room and stopped in front of the dresser. The silence was broken by the sound of someone biting into a gingerbread cookie.

Scott opened his eyes and leapt from the bed. He landed square behind the red-robed man, planted his feet and drove the knife high and hard.

The blade sliced through the man's coat and he dropped to the floor in a red velvet heap, not uttering so much as a gasp of pain.

The sleeve of Scott's SpongeBob pajamas glistened with new blood. He pulled the blade free and turned toward the hall, toward his mother in the living room.

When it was over...when the only sound in the room was the whispering *whirrrr* of the toy windmill Scott's mother set out during the holidays, his mother lay at the base of the Christmas tree, and her blood spattered the blue spruce in a dark crosshatch at its middle. Her eyes stared upward at nothing, reflecting only death and the blinking tree lights in their depths.

Scott sat with his legs crossed at the foot of the couch, three small pyramids of presents stacked in front of him. His expression was one of contentment. Satisfaction.

He reached for the first gift, his fingertips brushing over the silky wrapping paper, when he heard a thump behind him.

Scott spun around and saw a shimmer of movement in the fireplace. Flakes of soot and ash sifted down in a fine, shadow-like mist.

His heart flipped in his chest, and a louder thump came from the fireplace, farther up inside the chimney.

Scott scrambled to his mother, wrenched the fishing knife

from the side of her throat, and ran to the fireplace. He stood to the side and flattened himself against the wall beside the mantel.

His breath quickened. His pulse throbbed at his temples.

When the first black boot stretched free of the darkness, Scott smiled. When the second boot stepped onto the hearth and a fat man's body wriggled free, Scott raised the knife.

His aim was true.

END

BABY'S BREATH

She held the baby close, feeling its warmth. She pulled away the last button on her blouse to let its tender skin come in contact with hers. It moved puckered lips against the small of her neck, made a wet gurgle and she smiled. She closed her eyes and reveled in the details of the moment. Its heart beat, strong and rapid. The sound of its breathing, soft as butterfly wings. The touch of unblemished flesh and feathery hair.

Scent of diapers and powder. Even more subtle, the odor of the umbilical cord blackening in a crimped curl.

And the gentle, sour smell of its breath.

She wondered if the baby's mother wondered where it was yet.

IN COUNTRY

I'm in this hand job hut in North Philly, on the skirts of Chinatown, far enough away to not have attention drawn to the bad Asian signage on the front door and the blatant typo: Oriential Massage. The place stinks of old cum, damp carpet and dollar bin hand lotion. I hear the high-pitched nasal whine of a girl singing over whatever the fuck that stringed instrument is. You know the one I'm talking about… sounds like a cat being neutered without anesthesia.

I walk over to the counter. Some old gray-haired, Mrs. Miyagi is half asleep at her post. She stares at me for a moment, doing a slow blink. She looks familiar but fuck, they all look the same, y' know?

Back in the Nam, some guys went dinky dou cause they thought they were killing the same guy over and over and over again. After a while, it's no wonder some of us started taking ears and fingers as souvenirs. Not even age made a difference. Not really. Young boys looked like softer versions of the older ones. We were just killing them at different ages. Young girls... well.

Tiny little thing was my first kill. Four or five years old. Her feed sack skirt bulged from the explosives strapped underneath. When a man is faced with a situation like that, only two things to be done—kill or die.

Well… I didn't fucking die in the Nam. She was my first, but for damn sure, not my last. I caught her right over her left eyebrow. Opened the back of her head up like a can opener.

I sipped from the complimentary Sapporo beer as the young Lucy Liu came into the massage room. She was too thin, almost sickly. She smiled and nodded. Probably only understood ten words of English, all of them centered on how to haggle price. I nodded in return and she let her robe slide off to the dirty floor. Place like that, no need for discretion. You both know why you're there. I glanced at her arms and don't notice any track marks, so if she's shooting up, it's somewhere else on her body. I've had dirtier before, so I guess she'll do. She squirted lotion onto her smooth palms and smeared it around as I checked out her low-slung tits.

Her hands were nothing short of amazing. Her fingertips brushed against my skin like moth wings one moment, then expertly dug into my muscles the next. She was *good.* Good enough to get a *real* fucking job giving massages without the happy endings, but she didn't realize it. This is all she knows. It's all she'll *ever fucking know.*

It's been a while since I'd shot a decent load, but despite that, I felt myself start to drift off, more relaxed than I thought I'd be from the massage. More than I *should* be. I looked up and suddenly she was twins. The whole room was double. I glanced over at the beer on the side table and back at her. She gave me a smile, but not a nice one. I knew that smile. It was the same expression the Cong wore when they got through our defenses. The one they wore right before they blew themselves up. It said they knew they had you right where they wanted you and there wasn't a goddamn thing you could do about it.

Ol' Mrs. Miyagi opened the door and sat down in a chair in the corner. She smiled the same smile as Lucy Liu and silently pointed at the Ranger tattoo on my right shoulder, her smile growing wider. She *did* know me. From in country.

I couldn't even move. Whatever that slope bitch had put in my beer was doing its job. And when she pulled out the nipple clamps and the curling iron, I knew this wasn't going to be fun anymore.

END

IN DARKER WATERS

"The King is dead."

Emmett Stevens turned on the lamp and fumbled for his glasses on the night stand. "Who the hell —?"

"It's Smitty. You better get down to the lake."

"It's four thirty in the goddamned morning."

"Sorry Emmett, but you're gonna want to take a look at this."

Emmett let out a sigh, looking forward to his impending retirement. Small town or not, sometimes being the sheriff was a pain in the ass. When Emmett had taken office, sheriff Walder had handed over his badge and pistol with a smile. "Every day is like walking blind in a pasture. You never know whether you're going to step in a pile of shit or not." It was the truest advice Emmett had ever received in his life.

Emmett wondered if he would follow Walder's lead after he retired; pack up the roost and head down to Florida. *Probably not,* he thought. *Christmas lights wrapped around palm trees just seems... unchristian.*

"All right, Smitty. I'll bring a thermos of coffee for us." Emmett hung up the phone while Smitty was still talking.

"Everything ok?" Ruthie turned over in bed, shielding her eyes against the glare of the lamp.

"Smitty's rambling on about The King being... never mind, baby. Go back to sleep. I'll be back soon as I can."

He leaned down and gave his wife of thirty-seven years a kiss on the lips. "I love you."

"Love you too, hon." Ruthie turned back over and pulled the blankets tighter.

Emmett let out another sigh as he pulled on his uniform and gear. They felt heavier every day.

Palm tree Christmas or not, Florida was looking better

all the time.

--==•==--

Mist was rising off the murky water of Lake Branson as Emmett pulled the cruiser to a stop next to the loading slip. Wes Southard's pickup was parked halfway down the concrete ramp, boat still on the trailer. In the distance, the sun started to brighten the horizon. The maples and oaks on the hillside were becoming silhouettes.

Smitty crouched next to something bulky and glistening on the water banks. Tom Holloway was there too, but of course that was a given. The way Holloway gossiped down at the barbershop, there wasn't a mouse fart in town he didn't know about.

Fishing rod in his hand, Wes Southard stood next to Tom. Both men looked lost and confused. Scared.

What the hell is going on?

Emmett grabbed the thermos of coffee and some foam cups from the stack on his passenger seat and got out.

"Morning Emmett."

"Boys." He nodded and started to offer cups but caught sight of whatever Smitty was kneeling beside.

My God. What in the blue hell...

The King had already been a legend when Emmett was a young boy. He had never seen him firsthand, but there were countless tales of how he had busted line after line, escaping even the most skilled fishermen.

The closest Emmett had come was a few years back when Raymond Gover had driven his sooped-up Nova into the lake after drinking until closing time at the Wishing Well.

They'd had to call in an diver from Franklin County. Five minutes in and the man had damned near broken his neck getting out of the lake, shaking like he'd seen Lucifer himself. Never knew if it was true or not, but the man smelled like he had let loose in his wet suit.

Fact was, the diver had come face to face with The King.

The legends described the catfish as eight feet long with a mouth that could gulp down a basketball.

The legends were wrong. The King was bigger.

Emmett knelt down for a closer look and Smitty angled his flashlight so he could see better.

The King's eyes were milky white with death and as big as Blue Willow china saucers. Whiskers the thickness of corn stalks sprouted from the front of its snout.

A thick inner tube tongue the color of trading card bubble gum lined a mouth wide enough to swallow Emmett whole, and that was saying something. Lord knew, over the years, he'd had his share of second helpings at dinner and his waistline showed it.

But what held Emmett's attention – what made him understand the fear in the men's faces – was the rest of The King's slime-covered body. It was as big around as a grown dairy cow and would have easily extended a full twelve feet if it hadn't been torn completely in half.

The fish's spine had been shredded. Its skin glistened in ragged tatters around the stump of his body. One pectoral fin was completely ripped off, leaving behind a raw pink stub.

Smitty moved to aim the beam of the flashlight inside the carcass. Emmett could see the oily collection of The King's innards and was suddenly glad he hadn't had breakfast yet.

Emmett stood up and let out a low whistle.

"What the hell did this, Emmett?" Tom's voice was shaky. The man wasn't questioning for the inside scoop – he was scared.

Hell, Emmett had seen Tom and his kids jumping off the docks and swimming in these same waters barely a month ago.

Wes stared with wide glassy eyes at what was left of The King. Something in the man's expression proclaimed he was taking a break from fishing for quite a while.

Emmett took his hat off and stepped to the edge of the lake. A memory started to break the still surface of Emmett's mind and he forced it back down to the shadows where it belonged.

Smitty stepped up beside him, just out of range of the other men.

"Emmett?" he whispered.

Sunrise was about to break and soon the water would mirror the clear blue sky. For now, nothing but black ink stretched off into the depths of the lake, following the dogleg of hillside toward Bentley Springs.

Both Emmett and the lake had nothing to say.

--==•==--

Carl Mattigan shuffled down the hallway toward the kitchen, hoping Sarah had left him some coffee before she left for work. The house was quiet except for the sound of SpongeBob Squarepants in the living room. Robbie ate a bowl of cereal while his gaze stayed glued to the TV screen.

"Don't you ever get tired of SpongeBob?"

Robbie smiled and shook his head.

He's got my smile, Carl thought, returning Robbie's grin. *Eyes too. Boy's gonna get more ass than a barstool when he gets older.*

"Y' know, back in the day, Bugs Bunny would've kicked the crap out of SpongeBob." Carl feinted a punch to Robbie's stomach, making the boy giggle and reflexively protect himself.

"Riding your bike to school again?"

"Yep. After SpongeBob's over."

Carl winked at his son and walked into the kitchen. The coffee pot had a half-inch of weak looking coffee left in it. *Goddamn it, woman.*

Still groggy, Carl made a fresh pot, sat down at the kitchen table and shook a Winston from his pack. The newspaper was folded to the HELP WANTED section, Sarah's idea of giving him a nudge.

For Chrissakes, I only got pink-slipped two days ago!

Every year it was the same thing at Finnley Construction.

As fall approached, work slowed down until the lay offs began. This year was no different, just a little lighter than usual. But with the damned economy in the shitter, he couldn't expect to be busy. He and Randy Fuhrman had been laid off yesterday at quitting time. It came as a surprise, but after twelve years working a backhoe at the same company, it damn sure shouldn't have.

Sarah was trying to get him to find another job over the winter months, but what the hell for?

Screw that shit. I'll sit on my ass and collect unemployment for a while. Bad enough for nine months out of the year my back feels like it's going to fall apart when I stand up from the shitter. Having a backhoe jackhammering my goddamn spine eight hours a day ain't easy work. Let the government pay for a little winter vacation R & R. Sounds like a mighty fine idea to me.

By the time spring comes around, work will start up again. Always has. Always will. Sarah can just shut the hell up about it if she knows what's good for her.

Carl checked the status of the coffee pot and looked at the stack of dirty dishes in the sink. He tossed the classifieds aside and glanced at the front-page headline. Unemployment Claims Rise For The Fifth Month In A Row.

"No shit, Sherlock. You can add me to the list next month."

"What, Daddy?" Robbie called from the other room.

"Daddy's just talkin' to himself, buddy. Done with your Lucky Charms?"

SpongeBob must have gotten interesting because Robbie ignored the question.

A grainy picture of Wes Southard standing in front of the lake was on the LOCAL STORIES page. Carl read the headline and studied the photo. Slowly, he folded the newspaper and set it down on the kitchen table.

He sat there for a long while, his eyes glazed over as he became lost in thought. His cigarette burned down to the filter as it rested in the ashtray, then went out on its own. The coffee pot finished brewing and went ignored. Robbie came in with his bowl of cereal and Carl never noticed him.

Twenty-five years and it's back again.

Carl smiled to himself, and reached for the phone.

"Randy?"

"What do you want, dickhead?"

"Fuck you. We're goin' catfishin' tonight. Get your shit and meet me at the lake around nine o'clock."

"I'm on call at the fire station tonight." Randy was crunching something, probably those damned barbecue pork rinds he always had a bag of.

"Have them put you on call. Ain't gonna be a damn thing happenin' until Halloween and you know it. Then you're gonna be so busy you won't even have time to whack off."

Carl lit a fresh cigarette.

"C'mon, Randy. I'll get the bait. You pick up a couple o' six packs. Be like old times before we had kids 'n shit."

"I ain't got no kids."

"Only 'cause your wife's got an ice box for a cooch."

"I'd tell you to kiss my ass, but you're right."

"C'mon man." Carl took a drag, blowing smoke out for a dramatic pause. "I'll even bring the last of my stash."

The phone was quiet. Even Randy's crunching paused.

"Lyin' son of a bitch! You told me you were dry last week!"

"I know, but I only got a little bit and with both of us gettin' laid off who the hell knows when we'll be able to catch a buzz next?"

"I'll be there."

The phone clicked dead and Carl hung up the receiver. He smiled and shut his eyes in silent thanks.

--==•==--

Emmett leaned back in his chair, put his feet on his desk and started sifting through the photographs for the fourth time. They still showed him the same damned thing he'd seen in person earlier this morning. He tossed them on his desk.

When they got back to the station, Smitty had been

scraping up every last reason he could for what happened to The King.

Somebody's motorboat blade hit it.

A bear wandered out of territory and went after the catfish.

The King got caught in one of the water turbines at the dam and was cut in half.

Horseshit, Emmett thought. *All of them, horseshit.* He reached into his desk drawer and pulled a pint of Jack Daniels out, tilting it to the head for a healthy swallow before he stashed it away again.

A motorboat blade would have to be four feet long to be able to cut the body like that.

In all his life, Emmett had never heard of a bear coming down this far.

And the water turbines at the dam? No way. The King's body would likely be mashed to chum from all the pressure.

Emmett looked at his desk drawer, deciding if he needed another swallow of whiskey to deal with what kept coming back to his thoughts. He resisted the pull of the liquor and released a deep sigh, fighting the memory of what he'd seen twenty-five years ago.

Emmett felt himself shaking inside, fear snaking up his spine. When he admitted defeat, everything came flooding back.

A few months after Emmet became sheriff, his mother had lost an eight-month battle with cancer and being an only child, he had to take care of all the arrangements. It was a hell of a crutch to pick as a sheriff but he'd taken to carrying a flask in his jacket.

Ruthie had helped him as best she could, but Emmett was still in emotional turmoil. Relief because his mother was finally at rest, but guilty as hell because he felt relief. Anger because he had to do so many damned things before he could even let himself grieve. The night before her funeral, he had barely sat down with a bottle of Mr. Daniels when the call came in.

Kids had been swimming down at the lake. One of them, Tommy Mattigan, went under and didn't come back up.

Emmett remembered the call as clear as anything. The way Connie at dispatch had sounded. The fear in her voice. She had kids of her own and Emmett knew what was going through her mind. Connie quit not too long after that call. It took a certain kind of person to emotionally deal with all the reports to the station. He guessed after Tommy died, Connie realized she wasn't that kind of person after all.

Emmett couldn't blame her. One of the worst things about his job was telling a parent I'm sorry. No two words ever felt as inadequate in that situation as they did.

When Emmett got there, the two boys at the lake were scared shitless and in shock. The medics had bundled them in blankets and somebody had given them hot chocolate. The older Mattigan boy's eyes kept scanning the lake, searching for something.

They called in divers and searched the lake all the way down to the dam. Nothing. Not a goddamn thing.

Insult to injury? *Having an empty coffin at your kid's funeral.*

Emmett hadn't known the Mattigans, as they had only moved in earlier that year, but he went to pay his respects just the same. Hell, half the damn town had. It was one of the things he loved about living here. The people took care of their own.

Emmett sat in his cruiser for a while, taking swigs from his flask and working up the courage to walk inside. When the whiskey was gone, he went into the church, sat in the back row and listened to Pastor Phil talk about the Lord's newest angels living in the mansion of God. When Tommy Mattigan's mother broke into screams and crumpled into a ball in the church aisle, Emmett had had enough.

He slipped outside and went straight to a liquor store, upgraded to a fifth and drove to the lake, walked out on the dock and sat down.

Emmett took his hat off and felt the breeze against his

damp head. He thought about the two deaths in the past week. His mother, older, but still gone way before her prime. The boy, barely nine years old, sucked down into the darkness before he had a real chance to see life.

His anger grew until Emmett screamed out over the water, wordless shrieks of fury at God, life, death and the unfairness of everything. The justice of nothing.

Tears streamed down his face. He gave one last bellow of rage and lifted the bottle of whiskey to throw it far out into the lake.

That's when Emmett saw it.

On the far bank, a young doe stood at the water's edge. She must have decided Emmett wasn't a danger with the stretch of lake separating them, and she bent down to get a drink.

And the lake came alive.

Filthy dregs of muck at the edge of the lake unfurled into a thick mass the size of a Winnebago camper and dropped as a cloak over the slender neck of the doe. It *opened her up* and blood began to gush in torrents from the stump of her neck.

A tangle of rust colored legs was the last Emmett saw of the deer as she thrashed wildly and the dark mass pulled her under the surface of the lake.

Emmett could make out limbs beneath the muddy slick, rippled and lean with muscle. He dropped the bottle of whiskey and it thunked against the wooden dock before rolling into the placid water with a heavy splash.

It turned slowly and looked at him. There were eyes beneath the twists of water reeds and sludge. Glowing pupils, reptilian and ancient, calculating eyes that were predatory and patient.

Emmett pissed himself right there on the dock.

The creature submerged and Emmett watched as air bubbles hit the surface and a frothy wake began rapidly heading toward him. Emmett broke into a run, his back cold with gooseflesh and fear that he had only felt before as a young child. He made it to his cruiser and fumbled with the keys before gunning the car out of there.

He didn't stop trembling until he made it home and crawled into bed with Ruthie. She held him warm and close and ran her hands tenderly over his head when he cried against like a child. Emmett let her think they were tears of grief. It was easier that way.

Over the years he'd done well at burying the memory of that day at the lake, talking himself into believing it wasn't real. It was the whiskey, the grief, the stress of everything. Tears brimmed along the edges of Emmett's eyes and spilled down over his cheeks.

He knew better.

Emmett reached into his desk and took out the bottle of Jack for one more swallow. He couldn't look at the photos anymore. He couldn't pull out the yellowed newspaper clippings hidden at the back of his desk drawer talking about the Mattigan boy's death.

Ruthie's warm embrace and tender hands would never ease the hard facts. The plain truth was the world was full of monsters. The things that go bump in the night are real.

He took off his badge and laid it on top of his desk beside his duty hat, then undid his utility belt and folded it across his desk calendar.

"Good-bye, Ruthie."

Moments later, Smitty walked in to see Emmett still crying as he shoved the barrel of his service revolver into his mouth. A moment after that, Sheriff Emmett finally found peace.

Crickets chirped like toy whistles around the lake. Carl cracked a cold Budweiser and handed it to Randy, then opened another for himself. The Coleman lantern cast a harsh yellow-green glow over his face. He pointed to a cove on the far side of the lake.

"Let's head over there. I'll pack us a bowl and we'll get

things baited."

"Been a long time, buddy." Randy grinned and steered the boat where Carl had pointed.

"Hell yeah. When's the last time we went out like this? Shit...five years maybe?" Carl packed some weed from a plastic baggie into a small wooden pipe, lit up and took a hit.

Randy nodded and ran his hands over his scraggly excuse for a beard. He cut the motor and let the boat drift as he took the bowl from Carl and inhaled, releasing a plume of thick smoke.

Like most nights, the water was dead still. Carl looked around. They were roughly twenty feet from the bank and the glow of the lantern caught highlights of some of the trees. Maple leaves floated in the black water. Fire red and lemon yellow; a handful of party confetti drifting endlessly.

"Ever think about him?" Randy asked the question in a soft voice. He kept his gaze focused on his rod and bait.

Carl felt his heart thumping harder. He bit back a smile. He tapped the pipe over the edge of the boat and put it back in his jacket pocket. He took a slow, deep breath of fresh air in his lungs and exhaled the same way.

"Sometimes." He finished off his first beer and opened a fresh one. "Try not to. His birthday's hard though."

"I'm an asshole, man. I shouldn't have brought it up. Just being back here and all..." Randy cast his rod, staring out after it.

"Did you mean for that thing to get him, Randy? It got The King, y'know? I read about it in this morning's paper. Bit that ol' catfish clean in half."

"I don't know what you're talking about, man. Tommy drowned, that's it." Randy stared at the water. His fishing line shone like spider web.

"A stupid accident. That's all it was." Carl quietly turned his fishing rod around and gripped the shaft like a sword. "After you pushed him off the dock to save your own ass, did you see Tommy's face when that thing pulled him under?" Carl whispered the words. "I did."

Randy turned and Carl swung, catching him square on the cheekbone with his reel. The skin split to the bone, spurting blood down his face. Randy fell toward the side of the boat and Carl swung back again, catching him against the temple.

Randy outweighed him by a good thirty pounds, but Carl had leverage on his side. He grabbed Randy's right leg and twisted up and over the hull, just enough to tilt Randy's bulk over the side of the boat.

Randy gripped the edges of the frame as he plunged into the water, tilting the boat. Carl stumbled to his knees, trying to gain balance.

Randy reached inside, scrambling to gain purchase on anything he could find. His fingers caught the metal handle of the Coleman lantern and slammed it against the aluminum boat hull. The glow of the lamp swung wide, making the blood on the side of his face look like an oil slick.

"I'm sorry!" Randy reached a free hand toward Carl. "I didn't mean for Tommy to die. It was an accident!"

Carl lashed out, kicking at Randy's hand gripping the boat frame.

Sounds started building. Noises beyond the frantic thrashing of Randy's arms as he tried to get back into the boat. The rush of water. Deep burbling sounds of something rising from beneath the surface.

Randy's eyes grew wide with fear and his shrieks echoed across the water. He struggled frantically to climb into the boat.

Cold droplets rained down on Carl as he fell into the boat on his back. As it happened, he saw the creature explode from the surface of the water. It swung its arms, glistening flaps of pale wrinkled skin and purple veins the color of ripe eggplants.

It thrust up from the muck, parting the water in muddy sheets. Glistening leaves and wildflower buds stuck to its flesh. It swiveled its eyes downward and as Randy twisted to see behind him, he screamed.

The creature opened its maw and peeled mottled, salmon colored lips away from its mouth to reveal rows of discolored fangs. It shook as it opened its mouth, as wide as an oil drum, and descended.

Randy's grip on the boat slid free. He yanked the lantern with him and Carl watched Randy get pulled beneath the murky water. Carl glimpsed his face, open mouthed and screaming in his final moments before the lantern was extinguished.

Carl lay back on the belly of the boat. He stared at the sky and noticed the clouds had cleared. The stars were shining brightly. Everything was quiet.

He was still for a while, waiting for his heart to settle, trying to process the redemption that had happened. He reached for the six pack and opened a beer.

"To you, Tommy." He whispered to the sky overhead. "I love you little brother." Carl finished the beer and tossing the can aside, reached for the motor.

"Daddy!" Robbie's voice. Happy. A surprise bike trip to come night fishing with him at the lake.

Bubbles rose to the surface of the lake fifteen feet away from the boat. A wide "v" of a wake began rapidly moving toward the sound of Robbie's voice.

"Robbie, NO! RUN!"

Carl started the motor and gunned it, curling the boat back toward the docks. It was too dark to see the shoreline. All he could do was aim for the other side of the lake. The motor shrieked but Carl wasn't fast enough to keep pace with the creature moving ahead of him.

"ROBBIE!"

Carl drove the boat straight into the bank of the lake, throwing him forward onto the pebble covered shoreline. The motor, buried in the mud, sputtered and died.

Carl stumbled to his feet, searching in the dim light for his son. He ran to the docks. Robbie's bike was there, turned on its side.

He screamed his son's name but there was no answer.

Nothing but quiet darkness.

Carl walked to the end of the dock. The boards shone silver. He felt numb. He looked out over the expanse of the lake and sat down with his legs dangling over the edge of the boards. Beneath him, his shadow danced on the water's surface.

A flood of snapshot memories went through Carl's mind.

Robbie's first day of school. Sleigh riding. Learning to ride his bike. Trick or treating. Christmases. Birthdays. Watching Robbie dance to Led Zeppelin in Winnie the Pooh pajamas. Singing lullabies to him. Heating a bottle of formula. The soft, powdery smell of Robbie's infant skin.

The reflection of the stars rippled on the water of the lake. Carl leaned against one of the dock posts, and lit a cigarette from his pack of Winstons.

After a while, he started singing a lullaby.

And waited.

END

FREE RIDE ANGIE

"I've seen *a lot* of dicks in my day."

The heater started a low clicking and began to hiss dry heat into the hotel room. Angie pulled the drapes back and looked down at the street below, the brass horns and snare beats from the parade growing louder.

She didn't need to look at the reflection in the window. Angie could feel his gaze slide over her ass through the plaid skirt he had told her to wear, but who was she to complain? Angie had worn a lot weirder shit than a schoolgirl outfit, and his cash was green like everyone else's.

In the two previous appointments he never talked, only listened. Always paid up front, and except for a weak hug and the briefest of kisses on her cheek when he left, he never touched her; just listened to her speak as he sat quietly in his chair and fidgeted with his priest's collar.

"Got turned out when I was fourteen. Not unusual where I grew up." She watched the last performers in the Mummers parade as it came to a close. On the street behind them, a group of laughing college girls suddenly flashed their tits to a camera man, their nipples jutting out in the freezing air like muddy chips of ice. Angie let the drapes fall back in place, the teal and brown wave pattern blotting out the light.

"After I hit the concrete for my first ho stroll, I never looked back. First time's always the worst. It's not the pain of some trick bustin' your cherry, if you still got it, that is. It's not how scared you feel. It's facing the fact you're using that wet spot between your legs to live. I didn't start giving head 'til later, and after that, I was booked solid. Fourteen years old with cherry lips and the supine body of a young Nubian queen? *Shiiiiiiit,* I could have auctioned my mouth off at Sotheby's."

Angie looked up and laughed at his expression.

"That's right, honey, I know what Sotheby's is. Just because I make a living off body fluids doesn't mean I'm stupid." Angie smoothed out the pleated skirt and sat down on the edge of the bed, keeping her legs spread just enough to hold his interest.

"I got the nickname Free Ride Angie the first year I hit the street. One day I got home from school, place stank of hot spoons and cooked foil already, and my mom was curled up in the corner. Her boyfriend put his hands on me right in front of her. Not that she knew. Hell, even if she did, I don't know whether she'd have given a shit or not."

"I ran but I didn't take shit with me but the clothes on my back and my schoolbag. Crazy isn't it? Don't know why in the hell I grabbed my school bag. Ho's don't need to worry about passing algebra, 'cause countin' twenty dollar bills is easy math, baby."

"Lots of guys out cruising around looking for young girls. Younger the better for some of these motherfuckers. But those first few weeks for me were rough. I was so hungry. So tired. After my first trick, it got easier, but for a while, no one wanted to come near me. Thought I was a cop trap. I went all over the city, trying to find my way, looking for territory. And since I had no money, I gave the taxi drivers the only currency I had. Don't let anybody tell you different honey, a blowjob gets more miles to the gallon than an economy car ever will. It was four months before I had to pay for a taxi. So, Free Ride Angie I became. The lifestyle and the name both stuck."

"Last week I turned thirty-four. I spent the evening with my cat, two cheap bottles of Australian red and some Chinese take out, but two decades of dick tricks is something to condemn, not celebrate. Twenty goddamn years."

"When I started, there was Rock Daddy down on 21st and Walnut. He moved pussy and coke out of the old Sam Eric movie theater and carried a straight razor in his boot. Egg roll Sam had his territory down in Chinatown, but that motherfucker ain't even Chinese. I met some of his girls before. *Mean* bitches, let me tell you, strutting up at Arch and 10th, ready to cut your ass with a box cutter if you try to take their spot. Sam kept turning them over every couple of years, sending them back to Thailand and bringing fresh girls in. They used to cry so hard when they were going back. Most of them had regulars that were old 'Nam dicks looking to relive some good times."

"Never had me a street daddy, *huh uh*. You want fifty percent of my money? *Shit, baby.* You better get out your kneepads and Chapstick and help me suck a dick."

"It's all right though, I ain't complaining. This is just my place in the world and that's okay. I've turned more tricks than David-fuckin-Copperfield." Angie smiled a wan smile.

"At least that's what a friend of mine used to say. She wasn't a best friend though. Best friends ain't such a good idea for street girls. I've seen too many cold and stiff in alleys, spike still in their arm, juice in their veins gonna wet nothin' but the inside of a body bag. Hurts too much to have best friends."

"I never touch the shit myself. Never liked needles from a doctor, so I *damn* well ain't stickin' one in my own arm. Huh uh, baby, no smack for me. No coke either, unless it's in a plastic bottle from the S-Mart. Before I ran off, I saw my brother die from giving too many blowjobs to a glass pipe, so I don't be touchin' crack either. I'll just stick to my wine and smoke my mind once in a while. It helps me forget."

"I don't do nobody on shit neither. Not no more. Had me a trick when I was sixteen. I was so damn excited. He offered me six hundred Washingtons to go with him to a hotel room. By then I'd been pushin' ass for two years, and six hundred dollars sounded damn good to me. When's the last time you heard of a sixteen year ol' cooze makin' that kinda shake? Most times, they'll bust a nut in the first five minutes anyway, 'specially if they've got a dried up raisin of a wife who can't give head without her teeth. Those tricks get with a pro for the first time, that nut goes quick and you just might have yourself a new regular. Over half of them just go to sleep, and

I sneak my ass out of there, cash in my pocket, cum already dry on my lips by the time I shut the door."

"Well, this trick was different. We got to his hotel room and he pulled out a pipe and started getting wet right in front of me, damn angel dust making the air smell crispy, like someone had plugged in a hair dryer and let it run all night."

"Half hour later, black eyes, bite marks and my jaw hangin' off one hinge, I left the room, his cash in my purse, and the blood of murder on my hands. You ever see someone get a spiked heel slammed in their eye socket? Ain't exactly pretty honey, but let me tell you, it *is* effective."

"Somebody wants to have a few drinks, that's all right, but I smell anything other than booze on your breath, or see track marks on your arms, your ass can keep walking."

"Yeah, baby, I've had some close calls. The shit I've seen out here...it don't matter how many showers you take, you don't ever feel clean. I've been lucky though, mostly nothing but bruises, but hey, black and blue go together don't they? At least that's what the five-o around here say."

Angie leaned forward, looking at the priest. He sat there as before, hint of amusement on his face, hands folded neatly in his lap. The piss yellow light of the table lamp barely reached him in the corner and his black suit faded to shadow, leaving nothing but the glow of his gray hair and white collar.

"Honey, I know you pay me to sit here and talk, and I'll dress up in this school girl outfit or whatever else you want me to wear if that's your thing. If it gets your rocks off, I'm more than happy to stay for two hundred dollars an hour any time you want. But take your money back today. Let's say this one's on the house. And believe me, ain't nothin' tougher than getting money back from a workin' girl."

Angie fanned the money out on the bed and sat back, staring down at her hands. Suddenly she felt exhausted. The room smelled of stale cigarettes and hurried sex. She let out a long breath, trying to find her nerve.

"I need to tell you something, hear? I need you to listen to me because...I haven't told anyone else and since you're..."

Angie took another deep breath and held it in, letting it snake out of her slowly. "Well, I know you like to listen to me talk."

"With your tastes, you wouldn't know it, but when it comes to money, there's not much I don't do. Hell, I've even been known to mule a package or two for them Jamaican boys down on Southside."

She glanced up at him. "Don't look at me like that. Shit, honey, I said I don't *do* drugs, I never said I wouldn't carry 'em to put food on the table."

"Everyone's got their limit, y'know? You'll never really know who you are until you know where the line you won't cross is."

"We all like to think we're the kind of person that would do the right thing. Run into the burning building and save the baby. Be a hero. All that moral of the story, Dick and Jane shit."

"But most of us aren't. We look at the house on fire and walk on by, thankful it's not our home, not our kids inside and when night comes, we sleep just fine. Next mornin' we read the paper, to see if anyone died or not, and by our second cup of coffee, the whole thing's forgotten."

"Be a hero? Sorry, baby. You want white knights and satin, your ass is gonna have to go to the library. Heros are dead things and we all helped put them in the ground. Worse yet, most of us don't even feel guilty about it." Angie looked down at her hands, licked her lips and tasted the salt of her tears. "I never realized before last year, what my limit was. I guess no one really does until they're pushed."

"I was working the street and a stretch limo pulled up to the curb. Nothing unusual. You wouldn't believe the amount of rich Wall Street boys that have paid for some of my brown sugar. *Mmmhmmmm*, I do love those rich boys. They never haggle on price, they pay up front, and they cum quicker than any other type of customer." Angie laughed.

"By the time I'm just getting wet, they're finished, limp, and ready to pull up their zippers and run from the room, the thought of fucking a black street girl beginning to ruin what's left of their bourbon buzz."

"But when that limo pulled up and the window came down...I wish I could say he looked different, that he had somethin' in his eyes, or way of talkin' but he didn't. He looked just like every other whitebread rich boy wantin' to trade money for ass. Wasn't ugly, but he wasn't handsome. He looked like any other guy."

"Motherfucker rolled down that window and it *stank* of money like somebody was burning it for incense inside the car. I've been on the streets long enough, I should have known better. I *did* know, but when you walk the concrete for a living and a limo with soft leather seats and a mini-bar has its door open for you, instincts tend to get ignored."

Angie looked into the din of the limo and put on her best smile, ready to cast her sales pitch, but he put up a hand, free of callouses and tipped with glassy, manicured nails, and cut her off before she could speak, so she just kept smiling and waited while he looked her over. Most guys didn't bother hiding it. They took long looks at her tits and ass, watching how she licked her lips. But Mr. GQ Smooth was looking at her like she was a package that had been delivered and he was checking it over to make sure it matched what he'd seen in the catalog. He gave a smiling nod of approval and opened the door.

"Evenin' baby." Voice as soft as hot caramel, Angie slid in and let her dress ride up to show some thigh. He gave a brief, uninterested glance and turned to a mirror faced mini-bar.

"Cocktail?" A grin spread over his face, revealing perfect teeth Angie was sure had been made by years of braces. She returned his grin.

"You wouldn't happen —"

"Of course. Lemon vodka is a favorite of mine as well." His grin got wider and he fixed two glasses with ice, filled them halfway from a frosted bottle and handed one to Angie.

"Tricky, tricky." Angie smiled wide, took a sip and enjoyed the cold burn of the vodka, the citrus smell filling her nose and throat. "You a mind reader or something?"

He laughed, running a hand back through his blonde hair and Angie saw the gold glint of a Rolex. "Something like that."

"Well, tell me, honey, what's on my mind?" Angie gave him her best dirty smile and let her tongue flick out over her lips.

"Right now," he sipped his drink as ice crackled lightly in the glass. "You're thinking that for the first trick of the night, you hit the lottery. You're thinking you'll try to raise your price on me and I won't haggle because money doesn't mean anything to rich pricks like me. You're thinking I'll want nothing more than a blowjob or something kinky like having you spank my ass, and it'll be some of the easiest money you'll make this week."

Angie swallowed hard, her smile gone, and her throat suddenly dry. She brought the glass to her mouth with an unsteady hand and swallowed the rest of the vodka.

"You were also remembering you forgot to feed your cat before you left. But don't worry, right now he's eating the leftover lasagna you threw in the garbage last night."

No fucking way.

His smile full and smug, he reached out to steady the glass in her hand, refilled it without asking. Angie started to speak, mouthed nothing but empty sounds.

He sucked an ice cube from his glass. ""I'm a businessman. A dealmaker." He crunched the ice cube, showing his pearly white smile again. "I have a proposition for you. I think, in fact, this is a win-win situation for both of us."

Angie looked at the priest. His expression hadn't changed at all. He still sat stoically, hands folded in his lap.

The heater kicked on again, and Angie wondered how many times it had been the background music to sex purchased in this room.

"To keep clean on the streets, you can't be workin' without a rubber. Handjobs are one thing. Hell, napkins and soap will take care of that. But a street girl having sex without protection may as well use a razor to open her wrists and get it over with." Angie looked around the room and wished for a drink.

"In all my years on the street, I've only done it once without a rubber, and it wasn't by choice." She leaned back on the bed, propping herself on pillows and letting her shirt pull up to reveal the smooth skin of her stomach, the edge of her satin bra. "Big Haitian bastard with an accent so thick I could barely understand him. He paid, but he refused to wear a rubber and ended up raping me anyway."

Angie looked up and smiled. "Unfortunately I wasn't wearing spike heels the night I was with him or things may have turned out differently."

She looked down at her hands, watching the way the light played over her copper painted fingernails. "Didn't catch anything nasty, but his juice took hold and two months later I had to go see the scratch doctor at the clinic." She let out a long breath. "It's not something I'm proud of. In a different life maybe... Maybe."

Angie felt the hot tears in her eyes and tried hard to blink them away.

--==•==--

"I want to fuck you." The tinted windows blotted out the street lights, and his eyes looked black in the thin glow of the interior.

"Honey, I sort of figured that out when you rolled your window down." Angie licked her lips, tasting her lipstick and lemon vodka. "I know you ain't a badge 'cause they don't have the budget for this kind o' ride."

He laughed and shook his head. "No, I'm not with the police, though I do count quite a few of them as close personal friends." Leaning forward, he looked into Angie's eyes and she noticed again how dark they were, pupils and irises barely distinguishable from each other. "I'm willing to pay you a good deal of money."

"I'm listenin' baby, but money in exchange for what? I aim to please, but don't be askin' for any of that piss and shit stuff, 'cause I ain't your girl."

"Nothing like that." His expression softened. "I want to have sex with you." He held up one finger, manicured nail gleaming. "Just once. No condom and —"

"Huh uh, baby, no can do. Conversation's over." Angie grabbed her handbag and began to search for the door handle.

"You haven't heard what I'm willing to pay."

"Doesn't matter. I can't buy my way out of a death sentence with stacks of hundred dollar bills."

He reached into his suit jacket and withdrew an envelope and a folded sheet of paper, holding the paper out to Angie.

"The results of an AIDS test taken approximately four hours ago at a north side clinic. You'll find I'm completely clean."

Angie took the paper and looked at it. She'd seen enough of them to know it was legit.

"Good for you, but I don't ride bareback. Now let me out."

"You mentioned something about stacks of hundreds, I believe." He handed her the envelope, bulging at the seams. "You could consider this a down payment."

Angie looked at the envelope for a few seconds, then took it. At least half an inch thick, all of the bills had the wide, owl-like face of Benjamin Franklin on them. She had to be looking at close to ten grand. Angie felt her breath hitch in her throat.

"What's the catch, white boy? You can afford any piece of ass you want." The vodka burned in her stomach, and Angie felt flush, jittery inside. "You've got to want more than what's between my legs."

A grin slid onto his face again. "You're clean, Angie. You

take care of yourself and I don't need test papers from the clinic to know. You don't smoke, don't drink to excess, and you don't have a row of mouths on your arms hungry to taste a needle." His grin grew wider. "I want to have sex with you. Just once. And I want you to carry my seed. In exchange I'll pay you half a million dollars."

Angie felt her stomach flip. *"Fuck you say?"* She dug her nails into her legs. She felt as if she was going to throw up. "You want me to..."

"In exchange for half a million dollars, yes." The ice in his glass tinked again as he drained the last. "The payments will be disbursed throughout the pregnancy term, to...protect my investment, so to speak. Not that I have doubts, but sometimes money changes people in bad ways, and I wouldn't want you to do anything to harm yourself." He crunched on another ice cube, grinding it with his jaw teeth like gravel.

"Each month, an additional ten thousand dollars will be sent. At delivery, I'll deposit the remaining funds into an account of your choosing or I can provide cash if you prefer."

"Cash?" Angie felt as if her insides were burning up. "What about hospital bills?"

"There won't be any. You must deliver by yourself, alone and with all the fear and pain that natural labor entails." He licked the tip of his index finger and ran it over his bottom lip.

Angie heard the words but couldn't believe she was part of this conversation. "What if something goes wrong?"

"It won't."

She shook her head. "What happens if your bony, white ass is shootin' blanks or it don't take? Then what?"

He reached out and toyed with strands of Angie's hair, brushing them away from her face and touching the smooth skin of her neck.

"If you present a negative pregnancy test you'll still be paid. But I wouldn't bother preparing for that outcome." His eyes gleamed as if he had just thought of a dirty joke and Angie felt herself sliding into a dark place. "Let's just say I have faith."

--==•==--

Angie felt the tears rolling down her cheeks before she realized she was crying again, and she angrily wiped them away with the palm of her hand.

"Son of a bitch was right too. He never had any doubts he was going to get me pregnant." Angie ran her hands through her hair and let out a long sigh. "I knew it before he pulled out, his dick soft and raw from dry thrusting in me. I knew it the minute he came. Felt like the cold mouth of a roach was chewing, holding on to something soft and pink inside me."

Angie put a hand on her stomach, taking comfort in the pressure, the warmth. She looked up at the drop ceiling, brown chrysanthemum water stains bleeding through.

"It was a pregnancy most women would kill for. No morning sickness. No aches or pains." Angie pressed on her stomach again. "But that cold feelin' wouldn't go away. My tits started gettin' heavy with milk, and my belly kept getting bigger and bigger. Wasn't til damn near my due date that I felt it move. I could feel its fingers raking across my insides. Exploring. Looking for a *way out*."

Angie shook her head, tried not to let tears come to her eyes again, hating it, but helpless to stop.

"For nine months I stopped walkin' the concrete and traded g-strings and condoms for sweat pants and ice cream." Angie smiled but the expression faded just as quickly. "A whole month went by before I woke up and didn't smell sex on my breath, or feel it on my skin. I knew he was watching, keeping tabs on me. I never saw him, but each month I'd find a new envelope in my mailbox, fat with hundred dollar bills."

"One day with the money there was a note with a single word on it. 'Soon.'" Angie pulled a pillow to herself and hugged it tightly. Even with the heat still clicking it's air into the room, she felt cold.

"I've seen some bad shit with the life I've led. Lot of pain.

Lot of death. But I've never been as scared as when I read that note. I wanted nothin' more than to get it over with, just get on with a new name, a new life and half a million reasons to tell this city to fuck off. But I was so scared of what was going to happen next."

--==•==--

Angie stumbled as she walked through her living room and knocked a lamp to the floor, breaking in into long, gleaming shards. It was as if someone had suddenly dipped her in liquid fire and she screamed til her throat felt like it was shredding inside. It wasn't so much like stabs of pain, as it was massive, rolling waves of it coursing through her entire body.

The thighs of her sweatpants were soaked and her fingers came away bloody and slick with sour smelling mucous. Angie cried out as her abdomen began to tighten and she knew another contraction was building. She took off her pants and sat down as the steel band of pain began to constrict around her.

Angie knew it no longer mattered if she was ready or not. This was going to happen one way or another.

Right here.

Right now.

She stretched out on the floor of her living room and gripped the heavy wooden legs of her couch until she felt her knuckles creak in protest. Angie thrashed her head back and forth. The pain was unlike anything she imagined. She had no concept of time. It felt as if she had been having contractions for hours.

Her body was searing hot and yet she was convulsing from cold chills at the same time. The pain was all-consuming, transcendental. She felt as if she could lift free from her body and float away like an untethered balloon.

Sharp tips began pushing from the drum tight skin of her stomach as if something was forcing small, wide forks up from inside. Her muscles stretched and tore as small hands reached out from her vagina, opaque claws like antique milk glass dug into her labia as it struggled to pull free. A glistening head the color of rock lichen began to crown, framed by her bloody opening, and Angie felt her flesh grow thin and split apart as she widened even more. And suddenly, blessedly, the pressure was gone as she felt the weight leave her body in an urgent, wet gush to the floor.

Over her own exhausted breathing, Angie heard a brief, phlegmy cough and a sharp inhale of air, and the newborn unleashed its first throaty cries into the room. She turned to the shattered lamp and grabbed a slender shard of ceramic. When she looked back, it was already leaning on shaking, unsteady haunches and studying her intently with its wide, milky eyes, quietly chewing through the gray-green umbilical cord connecting them. It gave a low hiss, thin, liver-colored lips pulling back to reveal tight rows of thin teeth and a dark ribbon of a tongue, and Angie began screaming until blackness took her.

She woke to greedy suckling noises and the rhythmic feel of it kneading her breasts like a cat, its claws leaving bloody perforations across her skin. Angie looked down and it returned her gaze, blood and breast milk greasing its lips and chin. The pain from her crotch hit her in heavy, leaden throbs, pulsing in time with each suckle taken from her breast. Angie sobbed and it gave another hiss, ignored her and continued to feed.

--==•==--

"Father, I don't know if the sins I carry can be forgiven. I don't know if they *should* be." Angie rose from the bed and walked to the priest, sitting on the worn carpeting at his feet. "I've given the money away, every last cent of it, but I don't think it's enough to buy back my soul."

"I tried, Father. I prayed for God's help and I tried. I know who...*what* its father is. I tried to do what had to be done."

She looked up into his face and her voice dropped to a trembling whisper. "I just couldn't find the strength to kill what came from inside me."

The priest put a tender hand against the side of her face, wiping away the tears leaking from her eyes.

"I know, child. I know." He smiled. "Isn't he wonderful?"

His hands went to Angie's throat, clamping down his powerful thumbs against her windpipe and squeezing. Angie clawed at his face, pulling at his collar and shirt. It ripped open and she saw the black goat's head tattooed across his chest, framed in a thick red pentagram.

The priest smiled at her as he tightened his grip and Angie felt her muscles turn to water. Black phantoms danced at the edges of her vision and she could feel herself drifting as the room turned to a static blue-gray.

Angie yearned for warmth, for rest. She longed for the white embrace of light.

The world continued fading and as Angie felt her remaining strength leave, all she found, all she received, was darkness.

END

BREEDING SEASON

Myrna looked over thousands of ceremonial candles in the shop, admiring some of the more ornate designs. She had to find the perfect pair. Later tonight, after four decades with Drakba, they were going to consummate their marriage. Many younglings today didn't wait anymore, ignoring traditions of the old ways.

But *they* had.

By this time next year, Myrna would be bursting with hatchlings. She thought about tonight. Lit candles. Five glowing moons in the red sky. Warm grog and fine food. They would make love all night, and by morning she would finish devouring him to nourish her young.

BLOODLEGUM AND LOLLIKNIVES

Lindy tugged her patchwork gingham dress up over her thin waist and buttoned the straps over her bare shoulders. A braided crimson mop sat crookedly on her head, thick curls framing her face. She winked at Pudge, then turned to study herself in a broken shard of mirror propped against the living room wall.

Pudge's eyes sparkled with excitement. A moist lollipop stick protruded from his bow-shaped lips, sticky and glistening with lime green residue. His upper front teeth hadn't grown in yet, turning his expression into that of a smiling ferret. He was dressed in a black sweatshirt, his face painted like a skull. Deep shadows circled his eyes, and his cheeks, still plump with baby fat, had been shaded to create false hollows. Pudge blew a puff of air to get his bangs out of his eyes and rolled his lollipop from one cheek to the other as he watched his sister get ready.

Several candles cast flickering light around the room, puddles of melted wax at their bases. A stained mattress and a pile of dirty blankets sat in a corner of the room, smelling of urine and mold. Lindy moved a candle closer to the mirror for more light, and drew the end of a charred stick over her face. With a few deft movements, she turned back. Black asterisks surrounded her emerald eyes and a thick, stitched smile was drawn across her face. She smiled at her reflection, admiring her teeth, all sharpened to points over the last few months.

"Rag'dy Ann!" Pudge squealed and clapped, his stubby hands making sticky noises each time they pulled apart.

Lindy curtsied and waved her fingers at him daintily.

Ma and Pa would've been proud of us tonight, Lindy thought. *The night of the blood moon.*

Even now, Lindy missed them so much. But Ma and Pa had shown them the way, by Jesus. They had shown them the wrath of Cain and how, on this night of all nights, sinners must be washed in the blood of the lamb.

Lindy turned as Crispin trotted bow-legged into the living room, swinging a hooked cane in wide circles. He glanced at Lindy, then at Pudge, and tipped the slanted bowler derby on his head. The charcoal-colored suit hung loosely from Crispin's lean frame. Mustard stained his dress shirt and a black necktie fell past his waist. His baggy pants were dirty and torn, and tied around his waist with a length of cord. Except for a black smudge resting beneath his nose and two dark arches over his eyes, his face was powdered white. He wrinkled his nose and flexed his eyebrows up and down.

"Charrie Cha'pn!" Pudge giggled and clapped his tacky hands together again. He crunched down on his lollipop, making sounds like grinding glass, and spit his lollipop stick to the floor.

They look so handsome. Yes. Ma and Pa would be proud for sure.

Lindy shook her head and pushed away another pang of grief for her parents.

I've seen eleven blood moons. I'm the elder now. It's time for me to lead the night of the feed.

Through the boarded front windows, the torn plastic tacked to the outside window flapped in the darkness. In the distance, the glow of town lights rested along the horizon and seeing it, Her pulse quickened.

She began tucking what she needed beneath the fabric of her dress and handed plastic grocery bags to Crispin and Pudge.

"It's time," Lindy said.

"Time to feel the blood of the lamb," Crispin whispered.

They smiled at each other. Crispin blew out the candles.

Hand in hand, the three of them stepped into the night.

--==•==--

Ted watched as the repo-truck pulled away from the front of his house, his blue Jetta trailing behind it. He checked his pack of cigarettes. Down to the last one. *One way to quit smoking,* he thought. He shook it out of the pack, pulling it free with his lips. He lit the cigarette, crumpled the empty pack and tossed it to the floor. It landed among a cascade of unsorted mail, most with IMPORTANT NOTICE stamped across their fronts in bold red type. He kicked at the stack, watching as envelopes skittered across the hard wood floor.

Ted felt hot and tingly, as if carpenter ants marched through his veins. He ran a hand over his grizzled face and scratched the whiskers along his throat. Ted smelled the soupy stink of his unbathed body. He let the curtains fall back into place and pulled his bathrobe over his chest. The lights flickered and he paused, waiting for the electric to kick out, but it didn't.

Phone's out. Cable's out. Susan's out. And ain't any of that shit ever coming back.

Fucking-bitch-fucking-gold-digging-whore. Ted's mind wanted to continue, make a sing-song rhyme out of it. His stomach suddenly twisted in knots, as if he was on the threshold of a roller coaster ready to drop. Tears threatened, and Ted bit them back. He took a long drag off his cigarette and watched the wispy curls of smoke float up to the yellowed ceiling. He shoved an empty pizza box off the coffee table and grabbed a half empty bottle of Johnnie Walker, tilting it to the head and feeling its fire wash down his throat. He inhaled the last hit from the cigarette and flicked it to the throw rug, staring as fibers melted a dark halo around the glowing tip. The burning ember went out and Ted sighed, leaning back into the couch.

Among the folds of his robe, Ted felt the weight inside the left pocket. He put his hand inside, felt the knurled handle, the balanced weight, and brought the butcher knife into the open. He turned it this way and that, watching the way the light played along the honed edge of the steel blade.

A giggle burst free from Ted and the sound of it in the

quiet room startled him.

--==•==--

"Get out of the goddamned way, Gizmo." Ken nudged the Yorkie with his foot, and the dog yipped before jumping away.

"Don't you kick him!" Esther held an in-progress scarf to her chest. She pointed a knitting needle at Ken, scolding him. "You leave him alone. He's just a little dog."

"I didn't kick him. I just want him to get away from the candy."

Ken shook his head and turned to pick up the candy he'd dropped on the kitchen floor. He winced at a sharp lance of pain in his hip, *damned fall weather,* and put a handful of peanut butter cups in the plastic jack-o'-lantern. He watched Esther walk away, a gray-haired angel in pink curlers. Her tinfoil halo and inflatable angel wings wobbled to the sway of her wide hips.

"Goddamned mutt." He muttered under his breath.

"What'd you say?"

"I said he's a pain in the butt."

"You're a pain in the butt."

Ken bit his lip and threw the last of the candy into the jack-o'-lantern. He lifted a cardboard box from the kitchen table. It was filled to the brim with an assortment of comic books, trading cards of every imaginable sport, matchbox cars, and candy jewelry. If Esther had her way, she'd spend their whole damned retirement on Halloween night. Ken carried the box to the front of the house, stepping past Gizmo who blinked at him with his perennially leaky, puffball eyes. His powder-blue collar twinkled with plastic gems. A smug expression rested on his furred face.

Treats that damn dog better than she does me, for Chrissakes.

Ken feigned a kick toward the dog and it scampered out of reach. He smiled and set the cardboard box down on a table in the foyer.

"What're you smiling about?" Esther's face was pinched, suspicious.

Gizmo cautiously peered from around the corner down the hall. Ken turned back to Esther, his smile wider.

"It's Halloween. It's supposed to be fun. Trick or treat and all that. Caramel apples and candy corn. After all, this is your favorite night of the year, isn't it sweetheart?"

Esther's eyes narrowed.

"Go get your cape and put your fangs in. The kids should start showing up any minute." Esther threw a knitted white shawl over her shoulders. "And pour us some hot cider, it's cold in here."

--==•==--

Crispin flipped the quarter high in the air, caught it on the descent, and slapped it on his forearm. "Tails."

He and Lindy exchanged looks and Crispin shrugged.

Lindy sighed, closed her eyes and clasped her hands together.

"In Jesus' name, have mercy on those that giveth." Lindy's voice was low and steady. She opened her eyes and nodded at Crispin.

The three of them climbed the front stoop of a brick rancher. Its porch was lined with rows of potted flowers and a small bale of hay. A pumpkin with a crudely carved face, seeds spilling from its widely cut mouth, sat beside the front door.

It smelled earthy and damp, the way Ma and Pa's room used to smell.

Lindy stepped forward and rang the doorbell. A thin teenage girl in an oversized striped hat opened the door.

"Trick or Treat!" The three of them yelled in unison.

"Wow, look at..." The girl's smile wilted as she looked them over. She cautiously held out a plastic witches cauldron filled with candy.

Pudge reached in, withdrawing a tiny fistful. Crispin took

some next, and tossed the candies in his plastic bag. Lindy took her turn last and they bounded back down the stairs, mumbling thanks to the door closing behind them. Pudge was the first to dig into his treats, tearing a wrapper with his teeth and stuffing a spongy wad of neon pink into his mouth. He bit into it and pink syrup spurted from between his lips.

"Bloodlegum!" Pudge used the back of his hand to wipe the syrup, creating a bright smear on his cheek.

"C'mon Pudge." Crispin picked through the loot in his bag with indifference, and started walking back to the street.

A face peered through the frosted glass at the home's door, and Lindy saw the blurred shape of the striped hat. She smiled wide at the girl, waiting for the jagged angles of her teeth to register. Through the frosted glass, she saw the girl's mouth open into a dark *O*. Lindy spun and skipped to the street.

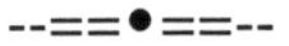

Ted watched the group of kids at the end of his driveway. A mummy. A princess. A dwarfed Spiderman in a plastic mask. Their bags bulged, heavy from a good night's score of candy. Even from here he could see their smiles, could smell the nauseating sweetness of their happiness. Their collective, joyful excitement made his stomach churn. Ted studied the faces of the ones not wearing masks.

So innocent. So... fucking... happy. Completely naive of what waits for them in life. No grief or stress. Faces unmarked with heartbreak or betrayal. No idea what it's like to have it all and have it taken away.

Tears sprang at the corner of Ted's eyes. They all laughed again, a high-pitched chorus. Ted heaved with nausea. He shook his head and took a drink of scotch. His vision blurred. They were all so beautiful.

I have to help them stay that way. I have to. How can I let them get hurt? Let them grow up, finish school and live the American Dream?

His tears spilled over, running down his cheeks.

Give twenty years of your heart and soul and they lay you off like you're nothing. Get married to a lifeless soul-sucking --

The tallest of the crew, the Mummy, stared at Ted and then glanced across the street toward the Dougherty's. Their fog machine belched mist across their porch. An animated rubber corpse popped free of its plastic coffin, and static-laden organ music drifted across the street. The kids turned away like a school of fish, heading toward the entertainment. Flashlight beams danced in the street as they left him.

Save them Ted. You have *to.*

The voice in his head came felt like something tickling the back of his mind. The words were soft, gentle like the tone of a friend speaking reason. The kind of voice you could trust.

Save them Ted. Spare them the pain.

Ted felt light inside, warm and bright, like springtime had arrived after a long winter. He had a responsibility. A purpose. More giggles spilled free from him. He put a hand over his mouth to stifle them, and bit down on his tongue as he watched the group of kids across the street.

Don't worry, angels. I'll save you. I'll save all of you.

--==•==--

Crispin twirled his cane and poked Pudge in the back playfully. Laughing, Pudge scooted away, dropping an orange Kit-Kat wrapper on the sidewalk. The lower half of his painted face was a smeared patchwork of colors.

"This one." Lindy pointed to a cottage house with an inflatable black cat sitting on the lawn. Stalks of corn had been tied with twine to the porch posts and rows of wax paper bags with candles in them lined the pathway to the front door.

Crispin patted his pants, making a show of not being able to find the quarter. He wiggled his nose, making his fake mustache move, and waved Pudge closer. Showing empty palms, Crispin reached behind Pudge's ear and produced the quarter.

"Yaaaaay!" Pudge screamed, shaking his treat bag as he tried to clap.

Crispin balanced the quarter on the tip of his thumb and flicked it toward the moon, watching its somersault winks as it fell again. Snatching it from the air, he flipped it over, checked it, and grinned at Lindy.

"Heads."

"Heads," Lindy whispered. Her breath quickened. Her green eyes sparkled. She put her hands together and shut her eyes.

"In Jesus' name, we shall be washed in the blood of the lamb."

Lindy reached behind her dress, feeling the comfortable steel weight she'd tucked there. The meat cleaver had been Ma's. Three blood moons ago, Ma had used it to wash Pa in his blood, show him his sins. And Pa, faithful as he was, had used nothing but his hands to show Ma the way. What a strong man Pa had been. But while they had still been alive, they'd shown them the light. The light of showing the sinner the sin.

She held the cleaver so the moon glinted from its surface.

Crispin let his plastic treat bag fall to the asphalt and walked toward the house.

The doorbell rang as Ken pulled two mugs of hot cider from the microwave and set them on the counter. He smiled at the "World's Greatest Grandpa" scrawled in mock crayon across the side of one of them. He listened for Esther and quickly opened a peanut butter cup and crammed it in his mouth, hiding the wrapper beneath some junk mail in the garbage can.

Diabetes be damned. This is Halloween.

He tied the string for his Dracula cape around his neck

and fitted a set of plastic vampire teeth into his mouth. Esther's sweater was on the back of a kitchen chair and Ken folded it over his arm and grabbed the mugs.

From the front of the house, Ken heard Gizmo barking wildly.

Goddamn mutt, he thought. Then he heard Esther scream.

Ken dropped the mugs of cider and ran.

--==•==--

They fell upon Esther like jackals.

Lindy straddled Esther's chest and sunk the meat cleaver into her exposed throat. The flesh parted and blood sprayed over Lindy's chest and legs. Leaning forward, Lindy caught some of the spray against her mouth. She clawed her hands and ripped a gold crucifix necklace from Esther's neck, then stuffed it into the gaping wound.

Crispin held a thick-soled foot on Esther's left arm, kneeling down as he pushed a knitting needle into her eye. The scarf Esther had been knitting unraveled like entrails beneath him.

Esther released an agonized scream. Her feet shook against the wood floor, beating a rhythm.

Crispin pulled the knitting needle free, angling it as he did, and skewered Esther's eyeball like a shish-ka-bob. It came loose with a soft sound like a champagne cork being popped, and dripped a trail of yellowish fluid across Esther's cheek. Crispin held the end of the knitting needle gingerly and tilted the bloody orb toward his mouth.

Sitting cross-legged beside the plastic jack-o'-lantern, Pudge held Gizmo tightly in his grip.

"Puppeeee!" He shrieked, and sunk his teeth into the dog's rear haunch. Gizmo squealed and tried to kick away, but Pudge bit deeper, peeling away a large patch of furred skin to reveal the raw bunched muscles beneath. Rich maroon flooded over Pudge's chin and neck, catching in pools along his collarbone.

--==•==--

Ken paused at the threshold to the living room. He couldn't understand what he was seeing. Esther must have fallen --

Oh God, tell me she didn't break her hip.

-- and two kids were trying to help her up.

But the red... why is there so much red everywhere? Even the damn dog is red. Had she dressed him up for Halloween too, for Chrissakes?

The little boy holding Gizmo looked up at him and smiled.

"Puppy," he said, in a tiny voice, and Ken saw the boy's mouth and chest were a glistening mess of burgundy. The boy turned away and tore another bite from Gizmo's back.

Ken began to scream.

--==•==--

Lindy and Crispin noticed the old man at the same time. Lindy howled and jumped to her feet, and Crispin scrambled after her. He slipped in a pool of Esther's blood and fell. He laughed, gave another howl to match Lindy's as she took the lead, scrabbled to his feet and resumed the chase.

--==•==--

Ken staggered from the living room and ran into the kitchen.

Oh God, Esther. Sweetheart, oh my God!

As he turned the corner, Ken slid on the linoleum, the puddle of spilled cider slick as an oil patch. The room spun wildly and for one surreal moment, Ken felt himself completely airborne. He landed sideways. His head thumped harshly against the floor and his hip twisted at an awkward angle. A bolt of agony raced up his side. The kitchen shimmered in

Ken's vision and, clutching his busted hip, he rolled over to his back.

The upside down face of a bloody Raggedy Ann stared down at him. She leaned closer and Ken could smell Esther's blood on her breath. The girl smiled wide and Ken gazed at the face of hell.

"Help me, Jesus."

"He sent me instead," the girl whispered, and raised a meat cleaver high above him.

--==•==--

Ted's heart hammered beneath his ribs. He shrugged off his bathrobe and let it fall to the floor. Sweat poured from his body, pooling at the base of his spine and drenching his thin t-shirt.

All saviors must experience pain to purify the soul.

He raised his forearm and dragged the blade across his skin. The pain, fresh and scorching, pulled everything into hyper-focus. The house was silent except for a distant tap-tap of something dripping to the floor.

Ted's blood created a chrysanthemum blossom at his feet. His mouth tasted bitter. His tongue felt thick and swollen against the roof of his palette. He reached for the bottle of Johnnie Walker and drained it, feeling the alcohol humming in his veins.

--==•==--

Pudge pulled the dog collar around his neck and buckled the ends together. His painted face was speckled like a red robin's egg.

"Cute little puppy." Lindy ran a finger along the collar's jeweled length and winked at Pudge. He barked in response.

A good distance away, Lindy could see a group of kids walking toward them. A tall boy was in the lead, wrapped in cream-colored bandages. He nodded at Lindy and whistled loudly.

"Come here little girl. I've got some candy for you."

She could hear the other kids in the group laughing.

"I'll be your Raggedy Andy!" More laughing.

Lindy put her hands to the meat cleaver tucked at the small of her back, then felt a gentle hand on her shoulder. She turned and Crispin shook his head.

As the group got closer, Mummy-boy's wolfish grin changed. The smell of fresh blood must have hit him first and confusion followed, a mixture of fear and doubt kicking in. He made eye contact with all of them, seeing their glassy-eyed expressions fueled by something other than a handful of candy. His gaze ran over the fresh, wet patterns across Lindy's clothing and the stains on Pudge's hands. Pudge licked red from his stubby fingertips.

Crispin put a hand to the rim of his bowler derby and nodded, smirking. The group's laughter died. Their faces grew pale beneath their garish make-up.

One of the smaller ones in the group tugged at Mummy-boy's elbow. "Randy?" His voice trembled, sounding small. Scared.

"Another time, big boy." Lindy put a hand to her mouth and blew a kiss. Her fingers wiped blood away, leaving four pale vertical stripes across her chin, and she offered her award-winning smile.

Mummy-boy's arms went slack to his sides. He dropped his flashlight. Lindy watched as the bandages wrapped around his legs grew wet with piss. The boy broke into a run and the others tore after him. The little one was half-crying, half-screaming, as he ran down the street.

"Yay for Li'ddy!" Pudge clapped and jumped up and down.

"This one's next." Crispin pointed to the house in front of them. It was absent of any Halloween decorations, but the porch light was on. The grass was too long, brushing against their shins as they walked to the front door.

Crispin flipped the quarter high into the air.

Craning his neck, Pudge watched its soaring journey.

Lindy's eyes gleamed as she studied its downward fall.

Crispin cupped it in his palm and slapped it against his arm.

Lindy and Pudge stepped closer and Crispin pulled his hand away.

--==•==--

Ted watched them at the front of his house.

"Come on. Come on up here." He held the knife at his side, slicing his thigh, mindless of the warmth spilling down his leg. He put his hand on the doorknob, and then pulled away, barely controlling himself from running out after them.

They laughed outside as Ted watched them. The boy in the baggy suit tossed a coin into the air and caught it as it fell. They studied the coin and turned in sync toward the house.

Ted's body suddenly felt electric. His heart labored in his chest as they began walking toward the house.

I'll protect you, children. I'll save you from life.

Ted trembled once. Blood slicked his hand and he tightened his grip on the knife.

--==•==--

As soon as the door opened, a cold, sick feeling, like she'd swallowed icicles and they had collected in the pit of her stomach, filled Lindy.

For a while, they lived in the house after Momma and Pa had gone with Jesus. When the men showed up knocking at the door, they hid, and when the men eventually broke into the house, they ran, leaving Ma and Pa's skin costumes where they lay. After that, the three of them moved around wherever they could. House after house. All different. All the same.

They made do with what they had. But God provided, yes He did. Ask and ye shall receive. He brought them men sometimes, unwashed and stinking of the streets, and they were thankful for His graces. They drank of His blood and ate of His flesh. Most of the men never even appeared to be frightened. Like sleeping lambs, they shut their eyes as they were fed upon and embraced death. Lindy could smell it on the men who tried to sneak into their homes. They stunk of sin.

Lindy could smell it on the man who answered the front door too.

He was somehow... *wrong*.

But Lindy was the only one who noticed. Pudge was still young, as excited about the sweets in his bag as much as he was about the feed. And Crispin, always the guard, was watching the street for any trouble.

The door squeaked open and just as Crispin turned around, the man lunged, grabbing Crispin's necktie and looping his fist around a length of the material. He jerked him inside the house and tried to slam the door, but he wasn't fast enough.

Lindy charged forward. Her slender body slipped through the opening. The man hit her with the back of his fist, sending her sprawling across the room. She landed on the coffee table, flipping it on its side.

Pain flared in her nose and lips, and Lindy could taste the brine of her own blood. Pudge latched onto the man's ankle, biting so hard his eyes were squeezed shut with effort. Pudge jerked his head to the side and peeled open a large flap of skin, exposing the gleam of bones. Screaming, the man kicked Pudge away. His foot caught him in the ribs, sending Pudge sliding across the floor. Pudge squealed in pain and hugged his side.

The man bellowed and turned back to Crispin, grabbing his throat and lifting him from the floor. Crispin's head thumped against the top of a door frame, and the man drove his knife into the tender underside of Crispin's chin. Sharpened steel sunk through bone and cartilage, upward through the palette and bridge of skull between Crispin's eyes. The blade sunk into the wooden door frame and Crispin's body dangled, impaled.

Lindy jumped to her feet, shrieking at the top of her lungs. She lunged and swung the meat cleaver at the same time, catching the man's spine right above the line of his underwear.

He arched his back and inhaled sharply. His eyes bulged in their sockets and his hands jerked out to balance himself, gripping the sides of the door frame. He stared up into Crispin's lifeless face.

Lindy jerked the blade of the meat cleaver free, the sound like a bare foot being pulled from mud. The man exhaled harshly, all his breath leaving him in an urgent rush and his body began to fold backward on itself. The white stumps of his severed spine ground against each other and the top-heavy balance of his torso lost the fight against gravity. As his torso fell backward, the skin of his stomach stretched and bulged against his inner organs and muscles. The cage of his ribs pulled his skin taught. His legs buckled and he fell sideways to the floor. The man released a low moan. His limbs twitched. His eyes rolled wide in their sockets like a frightened dog's.

Lindy stepped into his line of sight. She ran the length of the cleaver blade against her tongue, then raised it high overhead and buried it into the man's chest. The pressure made blood and body fluids burst out in a spray of scarlet. She cleaved through the man's chest, hacking at row after row of ribs to expose the beet-colored pulse of his heart. Lindy reached inside, using the edge of the cleaver to pry it loose from his rib cage. Lindy held the fresh organ in front of her. The front door was still open and in the autumn air, steam rose from his exposed heart. She saw the man's eyes, filled with terror. Lindy stared back, bit down and shredded away a thick chunk of his heart. Then his eyes stopped moving. His heart stopped beating a moment later. Lindy tore through the stretched arteries still attached to the heart, and wrenched it free.

Crispin's body, swung gently in the light autumn breeze. Pudge stood by the door, quietly crying. His bag of candy was in one hand, and he held his side with the other.

Lindy dropped the bloody heart to the floor.

Tonight was a night for endings. Tomorrow would be a day for beginnings.

"C'mon Pudge." Lindy held his hand and together they limped through the front door. With her other hand, Lindy stuffed the cleaver into her waistband.

Red and orange painted the night sky. The harvest moon smiled a bloody smile down upon her.

Lindy smiled right back.

END

MAGGIE BLUE

Maggie laid a crumpled wad of cash on the cherry wood desk.

Rupert swept his dreadlocks away from his face and glanced at the four crumpled twenties before turning his attention to the small mound of cocaine in front of him. He dipped the overgrown nail of his pinkie finger into the powder and snorted heavily.

Even from this far away, Maggie could smell the cocoa butter he used to burnish his dark Jamaican skin. He wore a wine colored shirt and slacks the color of Dijon mustard. Rupert snorted more coke into his other nostril and shook his head like a wet dog. His red-rimmed eyes gleamed. He traced his fingertips over the edges of his thin mustache and glared at Maggie.

"It was a slow night, Rupe."

"Yo' ass is fine as dis cocaine, though it damn sure ain't as pure." Rupert wiped the residue from his nostrils. "You don't have slow nights wid an ass like dat, Maggie Blue."

Maggie felt her stomach tighten. Rupert had been her street daddy for two months. He'd been good to her so far, but she'd heard him like this with some of the other girls. The edge in his voice, hard glint in his eyes. His actions were slow and deliberate. *The calm before the storm.*

"I'm sorry Rupe. I'll make it up. Tomorrow's Friday. You know I always do better on the weekends."

"Ya, I know." He sniffed and rubbed his nose again, then stood and walked closer. He kissed her forehead and slid his hand down to cup the left cheek of her ass. With his other hand, Rupert gripped the back of her neck and forced her to kneel on the floor.

"I know dat after yo' finished, yo' gonna get right the fuck back out on those streets and make some money."

"Rupe, I –"

"I fuckin' know you heard what I said, bitch."

His hold on the back of her neck tightened like a vice. She looked away from Rupert's face and started to unbuckle his belt.

He blind sided her. The sheer impact of Rupert's punch crumpled her to the floor and turned the side of her face into a raging beehive of pain.

Grabbing a fistful of hair, Rupert yanked Maggie back to her knees.

"Don't evah fuckin' test me. You ain't makin' money, den you ain't worth shit to me. Nothin' but a roach to step on."

Reaching into his pocket, Rupert withdrew a pearl-handled straight razor and thumbed open the blade. He held it at his side and the band of light reflected into her face.

"You behave yo'self Maggie Blue. Be a good girl, else I take one of dem pretty eyes of yours." He looked down at her and smiled with his wide ivory teeth.

Maggie saw black phantoms dance across her vision. Her face was already starting to swell and by morning she knew it would be bruised with purple crescents. She unzipped Rupert's pants and reached inside.

"Dat's right, you be nice to daddy."

Later, Maggie couldn't say why she chose that moment to make her stand. Maybe it was because she knew the first time a man hits you is the softest. Maybe it was the way she felt her body trembling, craving a coke fix, and hated herself for it. Maybe it was how Rupert referred to himself as daddy or the posture of his body, full of confident knowledge he could take his time and do what he wanted because she was never, ever, getting away.

Maggie chanced a look at the razor and gently took Rupert's limp penis into her mouth…and clenched her jaws shut with everything she could muster.

All the breath left Rupert in a heaving moan and his hands flew open on reflex. The straight razor skittered across the floor. Rupert screamed and flailed at Maggie's face.

Maggie shook her head like a mongrel dog and tore at his flesh. She clutched the back of Rupert's pants as he thrashed against her. The coppery taste of blood erupted into her mouth and behind it, a scalding spray of urine as Rupert's kidneys surrendered. Neither taste persuaded Maggie to let go. She ground her teeth together, feeling his flesh twist and burst against her tongue.

Rupert shrieked and went wild, punching and clawing at Maggie's face. He dug his thumbs into her eye sockets and she released him, allowing the flaccid, rubbery skin to snap away from her.

Thick ropes of blood and spit ran down Maggie's chin and neck. Her smile was sanguine. Rupert fell back against his desk. His yellow pants bunched around his knees, the material soaked with burgundy. His penis was mangled, shredded into pom-pom ribbons. It pulsed dark blood out onto his thighs.

"You bitch! Look what you fuckin' did to me!" Rupert bellowed with pain and grabbed a lamp from the desk. Maggie scrabbled backward on the floor, the anger and defiance she'd felt moments before getting replaced by tendrils of fear.

Her hands found her purse, its contents scattered on the floor, and she grabbed the first thing her fingers touched, raising an aluminum nail file in front of her.

Rupert's eyes bulged, gleaming with rage. White foam edged his mouth. His entire body trembled as he grabbed the lamp from his desk and raised the lamp high overhead and charged her.

Dreadlocks and blood streaming behind him, Rupert stumbled as his bloody suit pants fell to mid-shin. The lamp flew from his hand and shattered against the wall.

Rupert landed on Maggie at an awkward angle, knocking her backward, and he tumbled to his back and lay still.

For a moment, Maggie froze. Her eyes were squeezed tight with fear. Her entire body trembled, waiting for Rupert's wrath. She slowly turned to look at him.

The nail file jutted from his eye like a silver stem missing its flower. The pupil had been sliced vertically, exposing the pale inner tissue amid a pool of blood. Optical fluid glistened across Rupert's cheek.

Maggie looked away. Her stomach clenched, threatening to betray her, and she forced the sensation away. She took a deep breath, exhaled it slowly, and stood on unsteady legs.

The pile of coke on Rupert's desk looked pure and cool as freshly laid snow. Maggie pinched some onto the top of her hand and snorted.

She grabbed the eighty dollars from the desk and her gaze fell on a set of car keys. Rupert's Cadillac—a bright, shining example of metallic purple and American muscle. Slipping the key ring onto her finger, Maggie twirled it around. She looked back at Rupert's body, grinned, wiped the blood from her face and spat on the floor.

"Understand what a bad night is now, Rupe?"

--==•==--

Maggie turned the Cadillac onto the highway and looked at her reflection in the rearview mirror. She barely recognized herself. Hair, once long and blonde as corn silk, now a pixie cut of deep brunette fading to pink neon tips. Her full lips were painted a dark plum and her smallish nose had nostrils red rimmed from snorting coke.

And her eyes. Always her eyes. Bright indigo and so full of unspoken promises that her johns would sometimes get lost in thought if they stared at them too long.

If they only knew the pain swimming in their liquid depths.

Maggie felt tired and worn, so much older than twenty-three. Her daddy would've said that her soul was showing through.

Eyes like sapphire snowflakes, she dances. Her arms open wide, embracing life itself and my heart in her hands.

Maggie smiled. Her daddy's words came to her like silver

bubbles rising through murky water. *Daddy.* The poet. The lifelong romantic with a caring heart and a stern hand. How she'd loved him. God always takes the good ones. But at least she had him for twelve years.

As she drove, cocaine soldiers marched through her brain, shaking old ghosts free of sleep, and all of them whispered memories of Middleton, Tennessee.

The town where she grew up was little more than a few thousand acres of hillside forests and a smear of surrounding fields, a dark bruise on the pristine beauty of the Ozarks. Dirt roads crosshatched the area like cobwebs, dissecting land fragrant with the sweet scent of honeysuckle and cut hay during the summer. When the evening sun went down, the sound of crickets and spring peepers grew to a nightly chorus, and a cool breeze crept through the valley.

Middleton had a volunteer fire department, a police force of three, including the sheriff, and the nightlife consisted of watered down drinks at the town's only tavern, bingo at the fire hall or attending church socials with fried chicken and sweet tea.

They'd gather every Sunday, Maggie among them, to watch the church elders cite the scripture and show the faith. Some drank strychnine and called for the blood of the lamb. Pastor William and others would handle the rattlers, thick as a man's wrist, their tongues flicking in the air like lies from the mouths of evil men. Hellfire, brimstone, damnation and apple pie, and if it didn't have a banjo it just wasn't music. That was Middleton.

Just after Maggie turned twelve, Daddy died. Dropped to his knees in an apple orchard in late September, his heart giving out in one large solemn burst. After that, Momma fell in with mindless days working at the cannery, and nights sitting in front of the television. Her body and soul grew fat and indifferent to everything around her.

Maggie ran away when she was barely fifteen, though she'd buried her childhood years earlier, the summer Pastor William first came for her. After the first time, it was a string of hidden moments hiding in the shed where the rattlers were kept. While he had his way with her, she could hear the sound of the snakes sliding over their metal cages; their pungent reptilian odor, lidless eyes staring through her, tongues tasting her fear and shame.

Maggie learned both tears and prayers were a waste of time.

With the exception of her Daddy, Maggie had always been treated as eye candy on the plates of men, something to devour at their pleasure and excrete the memory of when they were finished. God was no different than the others and Maggie thought He was the most ruthless bastard of them all.

A few years after she left, she heard Pastor William got killed by a freight train one night; hellfire and damnation splattered all over the tracks. She still thought God was a ruthless bastard, but at least now she knew He could dole out justice when He felt like it.

She was so far away from that scared little girl from Tennessee. So far from her past.

Good fucking riddance to both of them.

Turning onto I-15 North, Maggie flicked a switch and the car roof began to retract. She slipped on a pair of sunglasses to hide her bruised eye, goosed the Caddy up to eighty-five and grinned as she felt the wind through her hair.

It felt like *freedom.*

--==•==--

The Sombrero Rojo rested at the base of a towering butte the color of wet rust, resembling an impatient, angry god. Maggie had been driving for four hours, and though the needle of the fuel gauge was just starting to flirt with the quarter-tank mark, she pulled in to fill up.

Sitting atop the roof was a ten-foot neon sign of a pinched-face Mexican wearing a red hat. His wide, toothy mouth blinked on and off, and Maggie couldn't decide whether it looked more like a satisfied smile or a grimace from stomach cramps.

As she was finishing pumping gas, she caught the smell of sautéed onions and skillet-fried steak coming from the building. Her stomach grumbled and Maggie decided the food was worth the risk.

She sat at a corner booth and ordered coffee and a breakfast burrito from the slick-haired waiter. The place was painted in vibrant yellows and greens, with flowing stripes leading to dust-crowned piñatas hanging in the corners of the room.

A single patron sat at a table on the far side of the room. From the look of him, Maggie guessed he was the driver of the idling diesel rig parked outside. He wore a red flannel shirt with an unbuttoned jean vest. A soiled hat with a creased bill sat crookedly on his head. He was skimming a newspaper with bleary eyes. The man glanced at her, gave her a nod and flicked his tongue out to wet his lips.

The waiter stepped from the kitchen carrying Maggie's breakfast plate. His long sleeved black shirt was a size too small, silver curlicues stitched across the front. He set the food down and Maggie smelled a mixture of cigarette smoke and tequila seeping from his pores. Despite the stink of the waiter, Maggie's appetite kicked into high gear. She grabbed the burrito, feeling the warmth inside the soft tortilla, and bit in heartily.

Maggie felt the crunching sensation inside her mouth. Legs wriggled against her tongue and spindly hooked lengths pricked the roof of her mouth. Cat whisker antennae flicked against her uvula.

Maggie gagged on the mouthful of food. She choked and fought against it, swallowing on reflex, and felt it slough down her esophagus, twitching all the way down.

"Jesus Christ!" Maggie yelled and threw the remaining burrito on the plate. Half a cockroach, the color of aged pennies, protruded from the egg and onions. It's rear legs spasmed and its insides spilled out onto a ridge of green pepper. White curds of eggs floated in a milky fluid like tapioca.

The doors to the kitchen swung open and the tequila-swigging waiter rushed through. On the tiled floor beneath his feet, black polka dots rushed around as if a child had thrown a handful of marbles. Maggie watched as one of them paused to inspect a fallen morsel before zigzagging away from the threat of footsteps.

The waiter ran up as Maggie pushed the plate to the floor. He started yelling in Spanish, machine gun fast, gesturing at the broken plate and food.

"El Cucaracha motherfucker!" Maggie ignored the litany of curses from the waiter and stormed from the restaurant.

Trembling with disgust, she started the Caddy and tore off from the parking lot. Dust clouds bloomed and she saw the neon Mexican in her rearview mirror. He looked like he was laughing.

The quivering feeling was gone from her throat but there were twitches of movement in her stomach. Waves of nausea rolled through her and Maggie forced them away.

The quivering antennae inside her stopped.

And other things began to move.

--==•==--

More than anything, Maggie hated to throw up.

She didn't throw up from getting drunk, nor from getting high and having the room spin a thousand miles an hour; not when she came out west and started hooking and gave her first blowjob; not even later on, when they made her do the animal flicks. She still hoped maybe the concrete jungle hadn't curled its way inside her too deeply, that the core of her spirit wasn't changed forever, setting her path.

If she had thrown up, maybe she would've found shelter from the storm her life had become and gotten a chance to start fresh again.

But maybes didn't matter.

--==•==--

The last of her coke buzz was fading, and the remaining light of day would soon follow. Maggie's bruised eye was throbbing with pain, and she felt feverish. Her stomach gurgled and she felt nauseous, but hungry too, which surprised her. After this morning's episode she didn't think she would ever want to eat again.

She flipped through how much cash she had left. Down to the last thirty-two dollars. At the rate the Caddy drank gasoline, it would be another day before she would be pulling tricks again just to keep driving. When she got back east, she would give it up for good—start over clean, stop the cocaine and leave the lifestyle behind. But right now she didn't care. Nothing clung to your skin like cheap, hurried sex. The thought of a hot shower and a soft bed were well worth the last of her cash and whatever price she would have to endure later.

Maggie pulled the car into the parking lot of the next hotel she saw and laughed at the Vacancy/No Vacancy sign. Out here, she never understood the need for them. In the desert, there was always vacancy.

The room was done in shades of avocado and rust. Sun-faded Georgia O'Keefe posters adorned the walls in thin plastic frames. There was a faint sour smell like old vinegar, but it was surprisingly clean and the price was perfect.

Maggie was tempted to collapse on the bed and make snow angels in the Navajo patterned cover until she fell asleep, but forced herself not to.

Her stomach was still grumbling. Starbursts of pain ratcheted through her in blunt waves. She had seen a vending machine at what passed as the hotel's lobby, and figured cellophane-wrapped food had to be safer than the cockroach burrito at the diner, no matter what the expiration date stated. A pack of Twinkies and some choice selections from the room's mini-bar sounded just fine right now.

Maggie fed her dollar bills into the vending machine.

She looked over the selections, her fingers hovering over the buttons. A shiver ripped through her stomach, and on its heels, heat suffused her entire body like a head rush. She held onto the machine for balance as she punched in the buttons.

A bag of cheese curls, a pack of Twinkies, and some crackers. *Dinner of champions,* Maggie thought. Her change tumbled down to the return, and she scooped up what was left. Thirty-five cents.

"Well now. Fancy seein' you here, sweet thing. You followin' me?"

Maggie turned and saw the truck driver from Sombrero Rojo standing there. He turned his head to spit into a Styrofoam coffee cup he held at the ready.

His face was peppered with gray whiskers, jowls in their infancy, their plump fullness beginning to surrender to gravity. His eyes were too small for his narrow head and set too close together, giving him the appearance of a poorly aged smiling possum.

A filthy green Peterbilt hat was on his head, its bill smeared with grease on one side. On his vest was an embroidered patch in red cursive lettering: DUGAN

He licked his lips and eyed her up, his gaze lingering over her body.

"You're a working girl, ain't ya?"

"I'm off the clock."

"I don't wear a watch." Dugan lifted both bare forearms to prove his point. "C'mon honey, I don't bite. 'Less you want me to."

He chuckled, and Maggie saw his lips were cruddy with tobacco juice. "I've got money. I'm headed back from a freight drop in Los Angeles and just got paid." He withdrew a folded sheaf of cash from his pocket. "C'mon, what do you say?"

The only thing Maggie wanted right now was to shower and sleep. She looked down at the odd-couple quarter and dime in the palm of her hand, then back to Dugan. Another couple of hours driving the Caddy tomorrow and she would need gas money again. Maggie sighed. Who the hell knew what tomorrow would bring? Money was money, and better the devil you know than the one you don't.

"All right, darlin. I'll give you a twirl, but you ain't sleeping in my room tonight, understand?"

He smiled and nodded wordlessly, his excited expression like a schoolboy getting special privileges, and followed her as she lead him back to her room.

Inside, Dugan spit tobacco juice into his Styrofoam cup and set it down. He grinned and wiped a wet smudge off his chin. Maggie unbuttoned her top and turned her attention to Dugan. She took his hat off and winced at the greasy feel of his hair, and he began unbuttoning his dirty flannel shirt. Unzipping his pants, Maggie pushed him back onto the bed. Dugan's stained tank top rode up over his gut, and Maggie rubbed her hands in slow circles across its girth, knowing he was growing excited.

"Goddamn honey. You are one tasty piece of ass." He sat up and turned, easing her down to the bed. "Wait. You first." Dugan pushed Maggie's mini-skirt, bunching it up around her waist. He moved closer, his bulk letting off waves of moist warmth and the curdled soupy smell of body odor.

Waves of feverish heat pulsed through Maggie's body. The spindly fingers of a headache were trying to get a grip on her, and she hoped Dugan would be the typical ten-second john so she could get his ass out the door and go to sleep.

He climbed closer and his breath wavered with the scent of steak and egg truck stop dinners and the minty stink of chewing tobacco. Dugan ran his thick lips over her neck, kissing her tender skin. Fat, sausage link fingers played with her breasts, pinching her nipples as his rough tongue licked at her flesh. A thin line of tobacco scented drool ran down her rib cage and he chased it with his mouth, lapping it back up.

He made wet halos around her belly button, and Maggie could hear his breathing deepen, becoming animalistic. Raising her legs, Dugan moved lower, using his mouth and tongue on her body. Maggie turned her mind inward, away from the sensations and the revulsion of being reduced to this for survival.

Dugan flinched away and coughed. He sputtered and let out a sharp hack as he tried to clear his throat, then hawked and sat up in bed. Maggie could make out the bulk of his shape in the low light seeping in from outside.

"Goddamn honey. I didn't expect no Paris Hilton, but clean the henhouse once in a while, would you?"

Maggie sat up in bed, and another dizzying roll of heat raced through her. "What?"

"You're so full of eggs, they're falling out."

Dugan coughed again, then grew still. "Turn the light on." He spit, and she heard a sharp slap against his skin. "Turn the fuckin' light on!"

Maggie flicked the switch on the bedside lamp and turned to look at him. Several pale, sightless larvae twisted in a smear of pearly yolk on the lower half of his face. Dugan wiped his chin and looked at the remnants in his palm. He screamed with revulsion, clambering backwards on the bed.

And the room's front door exploded off its frame.

--==•==--

Rupert stood there grinning. The setting sun blazed behind him, a fiery red nimbus making him hell made flesh.

"Been lookin' for you, Maggie Blue." He grinned and thumbed open the blade of his straight razor. "Been lookin' alllll over for you."

Dugan's whiskered face bleached of color when he saw the razor. He screamed again and the remaining larvae on his face shook free.

Grabbing a fistful of oily hair, Rupert flicked the razor at Dugan's throat, opening a wide crescent to expose tendons and yellow gobbets of fat. Blood fountained from the wound, soaking his grimy shirt and Dugan's eyes went wide as he clutched at his neck. He attempted to scream again, but the sound came out in liquid gurgles. Dugan fell to the floor, his fat belly and jowls flopping in sync.

"Maaaggggggggieeeeee." Rupert whispered her name, drawing it out. Patches of blood bloomed at the crotch of his pants and thighs, and he limped as he stepped into the room. A thin line of fluid trickled from his ruined eye and each time Rupert blinked, the flesh bulged from beneath his eyelid, making the skin look like a stage curtain gathered into pleats.

"We'll start wid an eye for an eye, bitch." Rupert lunged after her, the razor reflecting death in its blade.

Fear surged through Maggie. She felt weak. Sensations spread throughout her body like cold fire and her breath came in rapid pants. Her vision blurred.

Rupert squeezed her throat with one hand, bringing the straight razor to her cheek.

Her eyes rolled back in her head and Maggie's body grew rigid. Her back arched off the bed into a stiff bow as convulsions racked her body. Her hands and feet shook and thumped against the dirty mattress. Pink froth flowed from her mouth, spilling over her cheeks.

A flicker of uncertainty crossed Rupert's face and the last thing Maggie felt was his grip loosen as he hesitated.

"Fuck's wrong with you, you crazy bitch? You throwin' a fit or somethin?"

Bloody foam spewed from between her lips. Low guttural sounds reverberated from her mouth. Rupert leaned closer. Maggie's mouth yawned wide and her head snapped back. She released a deep groan, and from between her lips, the chittering noise of a thousand mandibles echoed off the hotel room walls.

Maggie *erupted.*

Cockroaches poured from her in a coppery black river. The pink mat of Maggie's tongue lolled to one side from the sheer pressure of them coming out. Several fought their way through her nasal passages and scuttled out of her nostrils like loose change falling from a slot machine.

Her sphincter gave way next, and a torrent of hairy

hooked legs pulled themselves free in a viscous wash of fluid. Her pubic mound swelled from the rush of them trying to exit through her vagina, still slick and glistening from Dugan's stinking saliva.

Maggie's body deflated. Her skin sagged against the frame of her bones. Rupert shrieked as they washed over him in an oily blanket, swarming up his legs and beneath his clothes. He beat the sleeves of his shirt and flailed his arms, trying to shake them free, but they swarmed over him, crawling beneath the cloth of his pant legs and scurrying up the outside fabric as well.

As they bit into his skin, the *click-clack* of hard-toothed pincers, miniscule but vicious, sounded like cereal popping in fresh milk. They crawled onto his face and reached his eyes, pulling on good flesh and damaged alike, and burrowed beneath his eyelids. As he screamed, they turned toward the source, skittering over his lips and onto the pink flesh of his tongue.

Rupert fought back, thrashing, trying to bite down, but there were too many, distending his cheeks and the sides of his throat as they tunneled inside. A cascade of ebony drowned out Rupert's last screams as they funneled into his mouth. He grabbed handfuls of them, squeezing and clutching their bodies till they burst open in white cottage cheese clots.

The roaches worked on Rupert, chewing and gouging at his body. There was a spray of blood as an artery was torn. Internal organs ruptured with showers of fluid, and the roaches filtered into the gaping wounds just as quickly, swimming in the soup of his body.

Covered in their numbers, Rupert raised his hand once, soundlessly, begging for something stronger than he, reaching for mercy from a higher power.

None came.

--==•==--

By the time they were finished, Rupert was nothing more

than a collection of wetly gleaming bones. His clothing lay in bloody shreds. His skull was absent of flesh and shining; buffed smooth by the sadistic kisses of a thousand mandibles. His blood soaked dreadlocks sprayed around his head in a matted halo.

Maggie's body began to fill again as the cockroaches retreated to their safe haven, burrowing into her every orifice. The pale flesh of her stomach bulged and rippled beneath the surface like marbles in a deerskin pouch. They streamed over one another to tunnel inside, the scritch-scratching of their legs over hard-shelled bodies. The last of them struggled its way into Maggie's left nostril, turned one last time to twitch its antennae and survey the room, then receded completely.

Her eyelids fluttered as she came to, and Maggie's breath hitched in her throat. She coughed and sat up, holding her chest. A greasy, rancorous taste coated her mouth, and a smell like melted plastic was in her head. Her body felt electric, vibrating inside, but replenished.

Dugan's corpse stared at the ceiling with milky dead eyes. His flannel shirt was soaked with blood from the gaping slit in his throat. She felt her stomach churn at the sight of the sliced, glistening flesh but forced herself into action.

Maggie knelt beside him and reached inside the pocket of his dirty jeans. Her fingers closed around the fold of cash and she pulled it free. Dugan no longer had a use for it and the Cadillac needed a few more fill-ups on the tank before she made it to where she was going.

She looked at the pile of carnage that had been Rupert. The straight razor lay unused in the bones of his hand. Maggie had no understanding of why, but she felt an odd satisfaction at seeing him that way, as if she'd completed some motherly duty.

Maggie picked the razor up and tucked it into the waistband of her mini-skirt, then strode from the room, leaving Rupert's remains to rot on the bed covers. Starting the Cadillac, she looked at herself in the mirror. Her bruised eye had faded and healed overnight like it was never there.

Maggie looked closer.

Her eyes. Always her eyes.

But not now. Not anymore.

The blazing sapphires she'd known all her life were gone, turned a rich, coppery brown, swirling with movement at their core. There was confidence there; deep-seated, ancient strength born of a symbiotic partnership.

Maggie left with the red blaze of the setting sun at her back. She smiled at herself and drove into the darkness that lay welcoming and waiting before her.

END

OF ALL EVIL

The residences of Wyntrebrook Estates were like a theme park for the wealthy. Even in the middle of the night, the swelled, egotistical pride of the people who lived here was evident. Bright outdoor halogens focused on the architectural details. Elegant stucco facades, trimmed shrubbery and manicured lawns, the massive, circus freak sized entrances with English ivy growing around them. The community was a who's who of stuffed shirts and rich, uppity snots.

A brown Ford Fairmont crept along, pausing at each driveway, one functioning brake light glowing in the darkness like a cherry on death's cigarette, then dimming again as it moved on.

"There's no way this is going to work, Darren."

click. click, click.

"And I'm telling you it is. It's the best selling garage door opener to these rich pricks. Byron told me like he was reading out of a manual, and Byron knows his shit."

"Just because he got A's in science class doesn't mean he's fucking Einstein."

click, click.

click.

"It's going to work." Darren let out a long sigh, then under his breath. "You're always so goddamn negative."

"What?" Mike glared over at Darren.

"Nothing."

"What'd you say?"

"Nothing, okay?" Darren stared back at Mike briefly and stopped the Fairmont again as they neared another driveway. Six foot brick columns framed both sides, gas lamps perched on top, brick walls flaring out to show off brass street numbers a foot high.

click, click.

The night air felt cool through the open windows of the Fairmont, but you could tell it wanted to tighten sweltering, burlap hands around your throat.

"I can't believe you bought into this shit. We're driving around in the middle of the fucking night waving at garage doors when we could be throwing back some beer and playing grabass with barmaids. Plus, I haven't eaten a goddamn thing all day. I'm starving." Mike angrily stuffed the garage door opener between his legs and reached inside his denim jacket, withdrawing a pack of cigarettes and lighting up.

Mike blew a stream of smoke in Darren's direction. "There's no fucking way this is going to work."

Darren stuck his arm outside again, pointing it toward another mini-mansion.

click, click. click.

As soon as he pushed the button on the garage door opener, he knew this was the one. He jammed the brakes and Mike jerked forward, mouth open, eyes wide. The three car garage door was starting to rise up.

"Son of a bitch."

"I told you. Byron knows his shit."

Darren killed the headlights and turned the Fairmont into the blacktop driveway. The closer they drove, the more massive the place became. Pale bleached brick formed most of the building, with huge block cornice pieces. There were the obligatory lights focused at the home's exterior, dark, shutters framing every window, and a small spotlight at the landscaped front walk focusing in on the high, arched entrance and the intricate moulding surrounding it.

"Who do you have to kill to live in a place like this anyway?" Darren eased the Fairmont up the driveway, watching for the houselights to go on. Nothing. He let the brake up enough to move a little faster toward the garage. They got within twenty feet of the garage, and still no houselights. Good sign. He looked over at Mike and smiled, throwing it in park.

The Fairmont rattled as Darren shut it off, the whole

frame trembling. Mike and Darren exchanged mixed looks of disgust and expectant rage at what was to come. A comically loud backfire belched from the Fairmont and it stopped the death rattle, going quiet. They jerked their gaze back to the house, holding their breath, waiting for the inevitable upstairs light to come on, shadows moving behind curtains.

Darren put his hand back on the ignition key, ready to crank it back up and haul ass. Still nothing.

"Hot damn. Empty nest." Darren checked his watch. 12:45. "Long weekend in the Hamptons maybe?" Darren grinned wildly at Mike. "While the cat's away..."

"The mice will ransack the fuckin' house." Mike laughed and reached to the backseat, grabbing a flashlight and two canvas duffel bags.

Darren stared into the open garage, lit by the dim lights of the overhead door. He popped the handle on his door, and then turned to Mike. "You sure about this?"

Mike clicked a flashlight on and off, testing it. "You're kidding right? It's your plan. You and Byron, that is."

"Yeah, I know, but we've never..." He looked at the looming nouveau mansion in front of him, and then back to Mike.

Mike turned to the garage, taking inventory, then took a deep breath and slowly let it out, handing one of the duffel bags to Darren and popping his own door. "Come on, let's go. I need cigarette money."

They put on gloves and started methodically on one side of the garage, quickly stuffing anything they could sell into the bags.

A pink tricycle sat in the corner of the garage, a bucket of plastic beach toys spilled out behind it. Mike grinned. "You want to take those for your girlfriend?"

"Kiss my ass." Darren reached into a cabinet, rummaging inside. Nothing but car care manuals and receipts. "Debbie's only four years younger than me."

"Might make her day." Mike went on, rubbing salt in the wound.

"Keep it up asshole, I'll leave you here."

Mike laughed and kept working the room. There was a mountain bike hanging on the wall and he reached out, touching the frame. "We should have brought a truck."

"Or a moving van. Yeah, that wouldn't have been suspicious in the middle of the night." Darren rolled his eyes and shook his head.

"Like your shit brown Fairmont's not? It looks like Sanford and Son in the middle of Beverly Hills."

"Man, you are just full of piss and vinegar tonight, aren't you?" Darren kept walking, working toward the doorway leading to the house. "Come on, let's make it snappy in case the Mr and Mrs are only taking in a late show."

To the left of the door was a small security panel with blinking green letters marching across its face. Darren read the letters and smiled.

D-I-S-A-R-M-E-D

Darren reached out to the doorknob, twisting and feeling the giving ease of an unlocked door. "We are on fire tonight." He pushed the door open and quickly stepped into the darkness, abruptly tripping over something and falling hard.

"Shit!" He rolled over on the floor, holding his right knee. "What the hell?"

As Mike shone his flashlight, Darren heard him let out a low troubled groan.

"We got some problems here, Dare."

Still rubbing his knee, Darren looked at what he had tripped over. A circular saw was in the middle of the tiles. The silver cast metal was bathed in deep maroon, and there were gobs of dark, clotted material still hanging on the teeth of the blade.

"What the hell?" The dried maroon continued on the floor to a wide, dark, path and as Mike trained the light on it, Darren's eyes followed it down a hallway where carpet started, and it continued around the corner.

"Let's get the hell out of here man." Mike put a hand down to pull Darren up. "This isn't cool. Something bad went down here."

"Look, we're already inside. If something went down, obviously the cops don't know about it yet. And I highly doubt whoever is still left here is able to call them." Darren looked back to the bloody saw. "Highly doubt."

Darren reached out and found a switch, throwing low light into the hallway. A skinny, wrought-iron table stood against one wall of the hallway with pictures on it, a small reed basket with keys and change in it. A picture of a tanned forty-something guy with dark hair swept back from his face, wearing a flowered tropical shirt and khaki shorts, smiling. Another of a Sharon Stone type of blonde with a girl of two, three years old tops. "The master of the house has done quite well for himself, hasn't he? Quite the trophy wife."

Darren walked on down the hallway, seeing the house open up to a vaulted ceiling over the living room. It could have been a double-page spread for Better Homes and Gardens except for the fact that everything was smashed up.

There was a sectional sofa lining the room, its white foam guts spilled out into bright, screaming clumps. Pottery was smashed in a corner, reeds of some kind tumbled from their gaping, patinaed mouths. A glass coffee table was shattered into long shards, tilted up like glittering punji sticks. Busted pictures dotted the carpeted landscape like photographic confetti. A big screen TV had a spiderweb hole in the center of the screen, zig-zagging out in wild, glittering lines. The ceiling fan overhead hung at an odd angle, cables ripped down from electrical roots, barely hanging on. Farther on, to the right of the living room, a counter top and the edge of a stainless steel fridge could be seen in a kitchen. A linen table cloth was pulled halfway off the dining table, several dishes and plates still there with food on them, others on the floor, a gravy boat, a casserole dish of shriveled baby carrots scattered like fingers of a jack-o'-lantern.

On the stairs leading to the second floor, the trail of dried gore continued up through the middle of the beige carpet.

"We should get out of here." Mike's face was solemn and tight. "Now."

Darren let out a low whistle, shaking his head.

"Don't have your smartass attitude now, huh?" He unzipped his canvas bag. "Come on, let's get started."

Mike watched Darren start walking toward the big screen and then slowly joined him. Once again, they began working the room, dumping cds and dvds into the bag. They were an easy thing to dump at pawn shops, and that meant fast money.

"Well looky, looky, we got nooky." Mike held up a dvd case, its cover showing a lithe Asian woman on her knees, lavender neglige ripped open. "Nothing better than dvd porn."

"Nice." Darren nodded, smiling broadly. "Too bad the big screen is all bitched up or we'd take that too."

"Sure, if you want a hernia." Mike kicked a broken figurine out of his way and grabbed a pair of silver candlesticks. His stomach grumbled and he looked to the darkened kitchen, putting his bag down. Glancing at Darren, he shrugged as he walked by. "I'm starving to death here."

Mike opened the fridge, casting harsh fluorescent light into the room and tapped his fingers on the sides, scanning the contents of the shelves. Withdrawing a plate, he peeked under the foil wrapping. London broil. Mike set it down and looked for something to drink. He slid open drawers and yelled out to Darren.

"Well, I'll be damned!"

"What's up?"

"Rich people besides rappers really do have a bottle of Cristal at all times."

"I'm going upstairs." Darren called from the living room.

Mike walked out to where Darren was, glancing again at the bloody streak trailing upstairs. "Dare, are you sure that's a good idea?"

"Will you quit worrying? Like I said, if anyone is still here, I really, really doubt they're much of a problem anymore."

There was a small alcove in the wall that held a mini bar and Mike grabbed a decanter, not even bothering to sniff the amber liquid, just tilting it to the head and handing it off to

Darren, who took it wordlessly, taking a deep swig as well. Scotch burned down his throat and a fireball blossomed in his stomach.

"All right, let's do it." Mike picked up his loot bag and took the decanter back again.

The stairs twisted up to the left and led to a small landing in the middle of a hallway, two doors to the right and the left. Mike tapped Darren's shoulder and pointed. On the left side of the hall there were four long, red smears like drawn out exclamation points. They culminated in a full, bloody handprint right before the first door.

"Darren, this is bullshit." Mike spoke in a low voice, sounding strained, ready to break.

"Let's start at the far end, check for jewelry and then we'll cruise, all right?" Darren sighed. "I guarantee you there's a Rolex in here worth at least five grand."

Mike nodded. "We check for jewelry and that's it."

"All right." Darren started down the hall.

The dark stain led straight down the hall like the stripes on a highway and disappeared behind the last door, cracked open just a little. They began to walk softly down the hall, easing their way, listening for any sound of movement, but there was nothing but quiet. Darren turned to the first door, motioning for Mike to go to the next.

At the foot of the door lay a stuffed, toy dog the color of Georgia clay. Across the front of its belly were several darker sprays of color and Mike looked away, tightening his grip on the crystal decanter as he edged closer.

He put his hand gently on the partially open door, easing it open so he could peek inside. Even with the dull light spilling in from the hallway, he could see that it was a child's room. Pink bears made a border at the ceiling, and there was a collection of stuffed animals huddled together at the foot of the bed. Still more on the floor. And there she was.

A golden spray of hair was partially hidden by a flowered bedspread and Mike could see one tiny hand stretched out from beneath. Half of the girl's cherub-like face was dark and bloodied, and she stared at him with one dull, blue marble of an eye. Mike's stomach flipped and he clenched his jaws together to fight back the urge to throw up, stumbling away from the girl and back out to the hall.

"Darren." Mike felt cold and sweaty and as if he could piss himself right here in the middle of a million dollar hallway.

Darren came out of the room he'd been in and looked at Mike, then his gaze dropped to the girl on the floor behind him. For the first time that night, the expression on his face read that they were way past due to get the hell out of there. He looked back up at Mike and nodded, trying hard to form words.

"Let's... let's go."

Down the hallway, there was a familiar whooshing sound of a toilet flushing.

"Get back!" Darren hissed the words through gritted teeth, and tucked himself to the wall. Mike crouched down low, gripping the decanter, ready to swing.

A man stepped from the end door, stopping at the head of the stairs, wild eyes shifting back and forth from Darren and Mike.

"Can you smell it?" His hair was splayed up all around his head in a stiff nebula. Dressed only in a pair of dark silk boxers and a white t-shirt, he was soaked in the same dried maroon that decorated the carpet and walls.

Darren blinked at him. It felt as if his heart was ready to throw a gear and burst from his chest.

"CAN YOU SMELL IT?" The man's raised voice was rough; work boots crunching on gravel. His expression hardened.

"I... I don't..." Darren's mouth was dry, his head felt like it was going to float away from his body.

The man's undershirt blossomed pink at his collarbone and ribs, the color seeping through from beneath the cloth. His face was a pristine example of scrubbed meat, his blue eyes sapphires on red velvet, and then Darren noticed his left arm, or rather what was left of it. Just above the elbow there was a belt tightly looped and buckled. Below the black leather there was nothing but the stringy, congealed remnants of a stump.

The man lowered his head and sighed, his expression softening, resigning his stance, as if he were talking to children.

He took a step closer into the light, raising both arms, gesturing pleadingly, and in the stump Darren saw a white core of bone like a center cut of bloody ham.

"All right. All right. I apologize." His voice suddenly gentle, placid, the man ran his hand over his face, back through his hair, matting it down only slightly. "I'm sorry. I..." He looked genuinely upset with himself, his eyes glassy, tearful, as he shook his head. "I forget that not everyone can notice it. My name's Gary." He began to offer his hand to shake, then stopped halfway, seeming to think better of it. Glancing down at the decanter in Mike's hands, he smiled. "I'd offer you a drink, but it seems as if you've found that department already." He gestured with his good arm, pointing downstairs to the living room. "Please, sit down. Bring the scotch if you want. I'd like to talk and I need somebody to help me. I... I can't do it by myself."

Darren backed up slowly, feeling Mike moving behind him. He had no idea what the hell was going on, but he desperately wished he was somewhere else; getting drunk at a bar, with Debbie at her parent's place, any-fucking-place-on-Earth instead of here.

Gary started ahead of them, strolling comfortably down the steps and walking toward the loveseat. Without even thinking, Darren started following him, shooting a glance at Mike, whose face had bleached of color. There was a split second where it seemed like it might work out. They'd sit down on the couch, play therapist for a while and figure out what the hell happened, and then leave, having one hell of a story to tell over lots and lots of beer. A split second. But when they reached the bottom of the steps, Mike dropped his bag and the decanter and started running toward the garage.

"Mike, no!" Darren screamed, but it was useless. The only

choice he had was to run along with him.

In the space of eight long strides they reached the door, but not before a heavy, metallic thump signaled the security system driving deadbolts home. Mike pulled at the knob, stepping back and kicking it.

Gary came walking around the corner, smiling.

One more fruitless kick at the door knob and both Mike and Darren turned to look at their captor.

"The alarm is top of the line, I assure you. Deadbolts on every door, shatterproof glass in every window." In his one good hand, Gary held a remote control for the security system. Cradled between his elbow and shoulder was an axe, both the pointed side and the blade darkly crusted and patterned, recently used. He tossed the remote to the carpet and brought the axe straight down, smashing the remote to fragments, then looked up at them again. "Please, I need your help."

--==•==--

"Three weeks ago was when it really started coming on strong." Gary looked down at his lap as he spoke, the axe handle propped between his legs. "It got so I couldn't even stand going into department stores anymore. The first time I noticed at all was about six months ago. I stopped at a BMW dealer and thought I was going to suffocate right in the fucking showroom. The smell was so thick I threw up in the middle of the salesman explaining why the 7 series is the best bang for my buck. Shrimp bisque right on his $120 shoes. He was so pissed off you wouldn't believe." Gary snorted laughter.

"This goddamn house reeks of it." Gary looked around the destroyed living room. "It becomes ingrained in you after a while, embedded in your DNA." He raised his stump, detachedly examining the ruined edges. "It takes a while to single it out, but once you do, oh sweet Mary, once you do, you can't not smell it. You can't go back to the way things were before."

Beads of sweat were fading lines through the caked blood on the sides of Gary's face, the hair at his temples wet and plastered to his skin.

Darren studied the room, looking for something, anything, that he could use as a weapon. There were canvases torn from the walls, gaping holes in the drywall like empty sockets where teeth had been ripped out. Frames smashed and broken, paintings torn in half.

Most of the coffee table in front of them had been shattered, but on the one remaining corner Darren noticed several dark clumps of material. It took him a few moments to realize they were steel wool pads, bloodied pieces of flesh still entwined in the metal fibers. He looked back at the raw mess of Gary's face and the ruined end of his arm and Darren's stomach lurched.

"What... is it that you smell?" Darren kept his words low and soft, trying to sound as calm as possible.

Gary looked up abruptly, looking surprised that someone else had spoken.

"The stink of greed." He shook his head and motioned around the room with his good arm. "It's infectious. You two, I think, are okay, but you can never be sure."

Gary walked to the big screen TV, lifting a picture of his wife from the top. "It's all through this place like a cancer, and by the time I found out we were infected, it was..."

"I thought we'd make it but then I smelled it on Lyn and that was the beginning of it all. It spread so fast." He put the picture face down on top of the TV. "I tried so hard to cure her. Nothing would help. No amount of scrubbing did anything. Scalding water. Bleach. Ajax. Didn't matter. That stuff's no use. The only way to cure it is to cut it free. If thine eye offends thee..." Gary gave a low laugh, shaking his head.

"I thought at first it was only in her leg and for a day or two after I took care of that, she seemed all right, but it came back. Lyn kept denying it even then, begging me to take her to a doctor. She couldn't sense it yet. But it came back so hard."

He turned to them both, his eyes were distant, pupils like dark pond water, dredging memories to the surface.

"It was in her skin, her hair, lungs. I'm sure that's how I got it. I could smell it on her sweat as heavy as a whore's perfume. I could taste it on her breath. I kissed her right before she went away." He put up his hand defensively, shaking his head. "I know, I know. Stupid of me. But Lyn was my wife. I loved her. It was just.. it was too late."

Gary's face crumpled in on itself and he released one deep sob before exhaling forcefully and hardening again. He vigorously shook his head from side to side, letting out a low growl and shaking off his emotions, sniffling hard.

He nodded at his stump. "Worst part of this? Washing my goddamn hands." Gary let out a harsh, barking laugh. "Or hand, I should say. But better this than the shit I was headed for. I'm just thankful I found it before it was too late."

"I got it just in time. That goddamn circular saw came through for me. Thank God I bought the high end carbide blade."

He snorted laughter again, waving his arms slightly and Darren got another good look at his stump, the bone sticking out like a pink exclamation point, the shadowy middle filled with clotted marrow. He strained his eyes to get a better look at the belt tourniquet wrapped around Gary's bicep and saw the stamped gold buckle. Gucci.

Darren felt Mike nudge his foot and he glanced quickly at him. Mike nodded in the direction where Gary had been sitting. He had left the axe, upside down, handle leaning against the couch.

"And Haley." Gary turned, chewing on his lower lip. "When you're young I think it hides itself better. It's intelligent you know? Clever how it works its way inside." He put a hand to his mouth, rubbing his lips, and then down to his throat. "Once I realized Haley was too far gone I made it quick. I already knew there was no way for me to save her. I didn't allow her to suffer, because after Lyn... after Lyn I learned sometimes you can't save the ones you love no matter how hard you try. Sometimes the only option is just to cut and run."

Darren tapped Mike's leg as he silently mouthed the words, "He's only got one arm," then gave simple directions with his fingers, pointing. *You go for the axe, I'll go for him.*

"But that's all in the past. We've got to concentrate on the present and the future right now." Gary turned to look at them and smiled a weak smile. And Darren and Mike jumped from the couch.

--==•==--

They lunged for him, and Gary snapped free, eyes wild, pupils wide and blown out like a barn owl's. He turned at just the right moment, twisting away from Mike's grabbing hands and jumping toward the axe.

Just as Darren reached for him, Gary swung the axe in an uppercut, sinking deeply into the side of Darren's hip. It pulled free with a wet, sucking sound like a boot pulling from mud and an obscene spray of red shot out. Darren shrieked and dropped to the floor.

Mike stumbled over the coffee table, the jagged blades slicing gouges in his thigh, and jumped on Gary, the axe falling to the floor as he dug fingers into the stump of Gary's arm, feeling crusted wounds and rough, wet bone. Gary's eyes fluttered like moths close to a light bulb and he fell to his knees, punching at Mike and making gurgling noises.

Grabbing the axe by the bladed end, Mike lifted it high overhead and brought the handle down on Gary's skull with a flat wooden thump.

Darren's hip was positively spouting. A gush of blood was ribboning out on the carpet in hot pulses, and Mike could see his face begin to change as he was going into shock. He pulled a pillow from the couch, pressing it down on Darren's hip and pulling Darren's hands up to push on it.

"Dare, hang on man, you're gonna be all right." He ran toward the door to the garage again, looking at the digital alarm.

A-R-M-E-D

"Shit!" Mike turned back, trying a door to the right. It swung in easily and the overwhelming smell of household cleaners hit him full force, along with the sweet smell of old death. It was a small bathroom, and sitting on the toilet was the lady of the manor, blonde locks of hair swept back, face ablaze and bubbling with powdered blue cleanser. Both accusing eyes were open and shriveled back in their dark sockets. Mouth a wide, silent scream, teeth and blistered tongue stained azure. The front of her lavender nightgown was splattered with bloody Morse code and the neckline and shoulders of her gown were bleach spotted.

Mike stumbled backward into the hall, almost falling, and a low, mournful groan came from Darren.

"Hang on Dare!" Mike looked up at the ceiling and saw a sprinkler system, then turned and ran for the kitchen.

The oven was a large, stainless steel mate to the fridge, and Mike turned every dial on the front, the gas burners firing immediately. Shrugging off his jacket, Mike pulled his T-shirt off and rooted around in the drawers until he found a spatula, twisting the shirt around and around, tying it, then putting it over the burner, watching the flames lick the cloth and catch fire.

From the living room the unmistakable, whining peel of a circular saw rang out and Mike felt his body go cold as he heard Darren scream.

Gary was standing with the saw, bending toward Darren's ankles when Mike tackled him from the side, screaming and rubbing the burning shirt into Gary's face. They both flipped over the loveseat, tumbling to the floor, the saw's screaming whine stopping as it fell. Gary howled, high-pitched and feminine, and began clawing at his cheeks with his good hand, the ruined arm flailing uselessly at his side, Gucci belt twisting and flapping like an exotic snake. Gary was rolling over and over, trying to staunch the flames on his face, and that's when Mike picked up the decanter with the scotch, sprinkling it over Gary like holy water and making the flames turn bright cyan and leap higher still. Gary began flopping in wild, heaving convulsions, his wails growing to a sharp, thin crescendo and then he was still, the flames and smoke rolling from him in grey, stinking plumes to the ceiling. It smelled of over-roasted hot dogs at summer camp.

There was a sudden loud pop overhead, and the sprinklers began to rain down on the room. A secondary thump, and Mike ran to the alarm again.

D-I-S-A-R-M-E-D

"Goddamn right! Time to get the hell out of here." He turned to get Darren, and that's when the door to the garage busted open, policemen and medics pouring through in a mad rush.

--==•==--

"What would you have done if the sprinklers hadn't kicked the alarm off? We would have been barbecued in there. Did that even occur to you?" Darren stared at Mike, waiting for an answer, a loopy, half smile on his face.

"You're always so goddamn negative." Mike punched him in the arm. "Besides, Byron's not the only one who knows things."

"105 stitches. You're lucky to be alive, son." The doctor walked into the operating room and smiled at Darren. He was bald on top, neatly trimmed gray beard and mustache hiding his middle-aged face. "If you had been hit at a slightly different angle, you would have bled out before you got to the ambulance, much less to the hospital."

He took a closer look at the long, vulgar gash in Darren's hip, the black stitches train-tracking along the edge of his pelvis. "You'll be in physical therapy, probably using a walker for a while, but other than that, you'll be fine. There was no damage to the bone, only the muscle tissue."

"A walker? I'll be the only twenty-something geriatric in the ward." Darren gave a weak smile. Even through whatever they had given him for the pain, his hip still throbbed and pulsed with a heavy, aching heartbeat of its own, but the doc was right. He was lucky to be alive.

There was a surgical cart beside him, rows of instruments neatly lined up. Darren didn't remember it, but people had been hard at work here. Wads of bloodied gauze were gripped in polished sutures. A bone saw, its blade still thankfully unblemished, was beside a pair of bloodied surgical gloves.

"The police will want to have some questions answered when you go to a recovery room, but I kept them out of the O.R. At least for a little while." The doctor smiled again, putting his hand out to shake.

Darren looked at the small rectangle of wire mesh window at the entrance door and saw a cop staring at him.

"Thanks." Darren grasped the doctor's hand and shook. His hands were smooth and clinic cold. "Thanks a lot."

The doctor walked from the room, pausing outside the door to say something to the officer.

"What the hell are we going to tell the cops?" Mike let out a heavy sigh.

Darren ran a hand back over his head and gingerly touched his bloodied lip. "Not too sure about that yet." He caught the fetid smell of rotted meat. It was foul. Rancid. A bloated corpse in the August sun. He jerked his hand away from his face.

"Dare? You okay?"

"Yeah. I'm... I'm just really tired." Darren slowly raised his hand up to within inches of his face. The stench was coming off his skin in rippling waves and he could feel the sickly heat there as it spread, marching through his bloodstream. His stomach boiled inside, empty, but threatening to force dry heaves before he jerked his hand away again.

He looked back at the doctor standing in the hall. The man smiled at him, raising his hand in a wave, and for the first time, Darren noticed the doctor was wearing a gold

Rolex.

A warm feeling of resignation came over Darren, and by the time he grabbed the bone saw and flicked the power switch, it was too late for anyone to stop the blade from doing what simply needed to be done.

END

PLEASING MARLENA

They were gathering at the front door again.

Richard could hear their dull thumps and persistent scratches and those liquid smacking sounds from their hungry, yawning mouths.

He knew he should check the peephole he had torn in the curtain, but right now he didn't want to see if they had made any progress getting inside. Seeing them during the day was horrible enough. Watching them scramble over each other in the blue haze of night was something he didn't think he could bear.

Marlena smelled of stale piss and rubbing alcohol. Blotches the color of overripe apples stippled her cheeks, and her eyes were dark troughs in a barn-gray face. Her pale lips were reduced to thin slashes of peeling flesh and the weak breath passing between them stank of approaching death.

Richard sat in a chair by Marlena's bedside, listening to her labored breathing and watching fluids percolate from the IV tubes snaking from beneath her blankets.

It was an awful thing to see her body wither away. She was becoming desaturated with life from the inside out as the cancer cells coursed through her blood.

Marlena's breath rattled in her chest, thick and phlegmy. Richard leaned closer, tenderly rubbed her hand and tried his hardest not to weep, silently praying this wasn't the onset of another coughing fit. The last one had been so violent that even after sitting her up and clapping her back to loosen her mucous-heavy lungs, Richard thought the coughing itself would take his wife right then and there.

But then she had hawked up something slick and gelatinous the size and color of a strawberry, and the coughing subsided, letting Marlena drift back to sleep.

He glanced at the night stand. Styrofoam cups lined up like sentries, dried brown teardrops at their edges and stinking of days old instant coffee. A pile of torn IV tags were there too; Marlena's liquid diet. Only three IV bags remained to keep her hydrated and nourished. After they were gone, Richard knew what would happen but like the creatures outside, he didn't want to face that reality either.

From downstairs came the sound of heavy metallic thundering and Richard quickly stepped to the window, watching one of them ram its head against the garage door.

The corpse's back was split open, bloody knobs of spine and the long gleaming fingers of a rib cage exposed to the night air. It pulled away from the vicious smear on the door and swiveled its head to look up at Richard. It opened its mouth, the flesh of its cheeks ripping apart and its lower jaw unhinging in a gush of black liquid.

In the moonlight, its eyes were wet shadows, but Richard knew its gaze was upon him. It released a gravelly moan and Richard turned away from the window. He glanced at the night stand to make sure his pistol was still there.

Marlena's eyelids flickered open like startled moths, and the edges of her lips curled up slightly; as close to a smile as she could muster. The gaze of her beautiful green eyes found him and he knew she was fighting to keep focused, but the effort was too much and her eyes gently eased shut again.

Richard reached over to wipe her forehead with a damp washcloth. He softly kissed her temple and brushed loose strands of hair away from her face. Two months ago her hair had been the color of spring corn silk. Now it was bleached of color, sandblasted and brittle.

He studied the lines in her face as he had done countless times before, and inside his head, Richard screamed at what had happened to her; what could have been helped had the end of the world not been taking place outside his plywood covered windows.

--==•==--

Everything changed when Plague 7 hit California. It had taken less than two months before the world had become hell.

All because one woman, a girl, really—she wasn't even old enough to drink in the States—had bombed a Chinese government lab in protest.

There was no way she could have known the contents of the building and what it housed—Plague-7, what the Chinese bio-technicians called the Crimson Dragon.

Nuclear reactors drew a lot of satellite attention. They were too difficult to hide beneath the global eye of the United States, so the Chinese had secretly turned to bio-warfare.

Plague-7 was a radically different approach, relying on combining DNA splices from viral strains and fetal tissue. Even after a decade of study, the research team was still stumbling in the dark, still only aware of the basics.

Far from destroying the virus, intense heat made it airborne, a fact the lab technicians discovered too late. It not only survived indefinitely in both fresh and salt water, but also rapidly multiplied in both environments, seeking any available host to invade. And once the infected host died, Plague-7 caused them to reanimate and seek other living things as food.

--==•==--

Easing his fingers from hers, Richard gently laid Marlena's hand down on the bed and stood to stretch. He heard the bones of his back pop and the pill bottle he had stashed in his pants pocket give a weak rattle. His foot nudged something beneath the bed and he reached down, pulling a chrome bedpan out from hiding.

Marlena's body was shutting down. A Hospice nurse had set up a catheter the week before the outbreak, and Marlena's body had stopped producing waste two days ago. Since then, the bedpan had stopped getting used altogether. Richard flicked the catheter tubing, watching the air bubbles scatter in the remaining urine.

Turning the bedpan over, Richard didn't recognize the reflection staring back at him.

He ran a hand over his face, feeling the crop of frosty whiskers, and realized he didn't remember when he'd last shaved. Richard thought and couldn't recall when he'd last eaten something either, but he no longer had an appetite to complain about anyway.

He was sure they were getting down to the last of what the pantry had to offer, although Marlena had always liked canning and the cellar had plenty of Mason jars filled with tomatoes and green beans.

Didn't matter anymore. Richard knew they would go uneaten.

Richard traced the crow's feet at his eyes, and the vertical crevasses bunched between his eyebrows; the telltale marks of a man carrying thoughts heavier than he should have to. His wedding band gleamed in the low light.

This September would have been their twenty-fifth anniversary; their silver. Why hadn't he been able to manage the years better? Spent more time enjoying each other, taken more vacations or...

The muscles in Richard's face crumpled and he felt his emotions threatening to erupt. He sucked in some air, held it, and shook his head, forcing the feelings away. Soon enough, Richard knew he wouldn't be able to stop them from surfacing, and the thought scared him.

In the den downstairs, in the front drawer of his desk, were two envelopes holding boarding passes and pamphlets for a cruise ship that he and Marlena would never be going on; a surprise trip she would never know about.

Things should be different. It wasn't fair.

Fury engulfed him and Richard clenched the bedpan, bringing it overhead. He wanted to slam it against the wall and flip over the night stand topped with its dismal rainbow of liquid medicine, old coffee, and magazines read ten times over. He wanted to shatter the glass windows and beat his fists bloody against the plywood until the nails screamed from their sockets and he could see the entire sky again; feel the breeze on his face.

But Richard put the bedpan down and sat, clutching his head. He could feel the ice pick rhythms of a headache coming on and the bottle of pills pressing into his thigh seemed to pulse, promising relief on many levels.

Not yet.

Not. Yet.

--==•==--

It sounded like one of those goddamn Sci-Fi channel mockumentaries they make to hype up a new movie. *Zombies? Bullshit.* But after a reporter with a live news feed filmed them stumbling through the streets of Beijing, people started to panic.

In less than a day, authorities reported outbreaks in a 120 square mile region. Three days later and the contagion had consumed China and broke free of its borders. By then it was too late.

When a country with a population of over a billion living people gets presented with a virus like Plague-7, there's no mistaking what the results will be. Earth had developed an unchecked cancer, and no treatment existed that would stop its progress.

Once the virus hit North Korea, Kim Jong-un organized the military and tried to dispatch as many of the walking dead as he could. Using his own people for bait, he herded the dead into tanker ships, turned off their beacon signals, and sent them out to sea.

Kim Jong-un will rot in hell for what he's done.

When a tanker came skidding on shore in the Lost Coast of California, no one from Homeland Security even saw it coming.

Some young, next-new-thing Hollywood director had production set up on the coastline making a film when the first attack happened. One of the sound crew was filmed having his liver eaten in hi-definition and chaos erupted as the rest of the set was overrun.

The next evening, *Entertainment Tonight* ran exclusive footage of Ashton Kutcher getting his throat torn out by an elderly Korean man and a schoolgirl of no more than nine staggering off with what looked like a chunk of kidney and a leaking, ragged section of intestine.

When it reached Seattle, CNN's remote tower cameras showed a young brunette with half her face melted. She was wearing a bloody Starbucks apron and sat Indian style on the sidewalk, a severed head cradled in her lap. She kept dipping her fingers into a crushed section of the man's skull, drawing out what looked like pink ambrosia, and sucking it from her fingers.

--==•==--

Marlena made raspy, dry sounds with her mouth, and tried to lick her lips. Richard withdrew the straw from her untouched glass, capping the end with his thumb to trap the water inside. He held the straw over her lips and let some of the water dribble out to moisten them.

He put the straw back and looked into the glass. The microbes were too small to see but Richard tried just the same. Just before the TV signals had stopped, Plague-7 had hit the public water supply, and he knew it flowed through the pipes into his house. Like most everything else, that didn't really matter anymore either.

--==•==--

Looting, taking place almost everywhere, leapt to riot proportions, leaving people dying in every way, shape and form. Gun sales skyrocketed to where background checks overloaded the system and customers began shooting the clerks and stealing the weapons.

Total break down of society had happened in less than a month. Martial Law was enforced. The National Guard was called out, quickly followed by the Marines and every available soldier of all branches, but it was too little, too late. The endless supply of the dead kept coming and coming, and coming.

Richard was sure the core government was still intact, pocketed away beneath some dank mountain somewhere, waiting things out. But he doubted their waiting would ever end. It's hard to compete with the patience of the dead.

Radio stations went off the air one by one, leaving white noise in their wake. To their credit, CNN was the last TV station to continue broadcasting, but in the third week it showed nothing but a side angle of the news anchor's desk, bright blue lights on the panels behind it, as if the camera man had overturned his equipment and left. It stayed like that for about a day and a half and then it was nothing but static.

After that...there was nothing but the dead.

--==•==--

Richard had gathered medications for Marlena then resigned himself to boarding up the house and waiting for something to happen.

It was a matter of time.

Eventually the electric would kick out. Eventually the water would stop flowing into the house. Eventually Marlena would die, awaken again, and hunger as they did outside.

Eventually.

He picked up his pistol held it to his nose, sniffed the gun oil. He looked into the gaping .45 caliber barrel and then at Marlena.

Richard pressed his palms hard into his eyes, trying to staunch the thoughts in his head, making bright flashes dance in his vision, clenching his jaws tightly together.

Richard wished he was a stronger man, capable of putting

a bullet in Marlena's head, and sparing her the aftermath. But he couldn't.

He pressed the clip release, feeling its weight pop into the palm of his hand, and began pushing the bullets free with his thumb. Each round hit the hardwood floor and rolled in fat, lazy arcs. The last round fell and Richard watched the dull brass casing roll beneath the bed.

Marlena stopped breathing.

Richard snapped his head up and looked at her face; saw the worn lines smooth out, her muscles relax.

His world imploded. Richard crumbled into a heap on the floor. He held Marlena's hand against the side of his face, and curled his other arm around his knees. Rocking himself. Sobbing. Screaming the tears he had held off for so long.

Richard wept for children they had postponed until it was so late in life it seemed foolish to entertain the thought anymore. He wept for things they had never done and dinners he was late for, too many late nights at the office, and not saying I love you more often. He wept because he could have done more when he had the chance, and hadn't.

Richard stayed that way until the tears subsided. He used his sleeve to wipe his face and settled into his chair again, reaching deep into his pockets to withdraw the pill bottle.

He had tried to make Marlena happy as best he could for the years they had been together. That's what couples were supposed to do—make each other happy. If it was in his power to fulfill a request from her, he did it—no questions asked. Oh, they had had quarrels like every couple does, sometimes real screaming matches, but after the storms passed, they always went back to square one—never holding grudges, the true meaning of mates.

Richard looked down at his wedding band, then at Marlena's. She had lost weight so rapidly her finger wouldn't keep her ring on anymore, and she had cried about it, insisted when she was still coherent that Richard wind yarn around the band to thicken it up and make it fit. He remembered her beaming, resurrected smile when he put it snugly back on her finger again.

He always did love to see her smile. Taking her hand, Richard put it to the side of his face again, feeling her soft skin beginning to cool already, losing what little warmth it held. He set her hand gently back to the mattress.

Uncapping the bottle, Richard began to dump the Darvon into his palm, but turned and shook them into his mouth like a child emptying a box of candy. He chewed them; the acidic taste coating his mouth, and he forced some beneath his tongue, wanting them to hit his bloodstream as fast as possible.

He tilted the amber bottle again, letting the remaining pills tumble into his mouth, and Richard crunched them all, swallowing them in three gulps and rinsing his mouth with cold coffee from the night stand.

Downstairs, he could hear the sounds of them battering the front door again. Nails squealed from their position in the oak door frame. Splintering wood.

Richard climbed into Marlena's bed and lay down beside her. His body was starting to tingle, and Richard smiled, glad the pills were taking hold. Everything was beginning to feel sharper and out of focus at the same time. Closing his eyes, Richard caught the faint scent of Marlena's hair; the lilac shampoo she liked. His hands began to flex involuntarily, bunching the down quilt in his fists.

There were more noises but they seemed to be coming from farther away. The sound of moist bones grinding in dry sockets. Something wet and leaden falling to the plush carpet.

The tingling grew to an electric buzz and Richard felt it rushing through his veins. He tried to move and it felt as if his arms had floated away like balloons from the butter slick fingers of a child.

He could smell the heady, fetid odor of decaying meat, so thick Richard could taste it in his mouth like rancid syrup. He heard the low, whistling tremor of air passing through dead vocal chords.

Richard opened his eyes one last time to look at Marlena, and he saw her staring back at him, the brilliant emerald green of her eyes now murky and lifeless, absent of emotion.

Richard felt himself drifting into a comforting black void. Marlena nuzzled his shoulder, moving her breathless mouth against his neck, tonguing the tender flesh and making soft mewling noises.

There was a stinging, ripping pressure at his throat, and a warm, pulsing release. Richard let himself go, knowing Marlena would be pleased.

END

GEORGIE

I think if it was only the death of our son, Maria and I would've made it, y'know? Picked each other up and worked through the grief. Healed each other. Saved our marriage.

Maria was the love of my life. Even now, after everything that's happened, there are days when I still miss her so much. I used to be angry at her for leaving, but not anymore. Not really. I know she loved me. I understand.

See, the thing is, my wife didn't leave because our son *died*.

She left because he *came back*.

--==•==--

You ever see those couples that are effortless?

You know the kind. They finish each other's sentences, reach for each other's hands like they have magnets in their palms. They just seem to *mesh* with each other.

Maria and I never had that.

We really had to work at our marriage but I was okay with that, y'know? It damn sure wasn't love at first sight. I thought she was just another rich girl riding Daddy's coattails and she thought I was some Irish street punk with a future of scams and back alley hustles. Hell, the thing is, that's probably the life I'd be leading if I hadn't met her. It was what I grew up knowing. After I met Maria I started to think I could rise up from the streets and make something of myself.

Maria was beautiful. She looked like some east coast cheerleader when I met her. Silky brunette hair pulled back in a ponytail. Innocent eyes set in a pure face. I don't know what the hell she saw in me. When we fell for each other, we *fell hard.* Sometimes, I loved her so much it hurt.

We tied the knot about a year after we met, both of us young as hell, trying to carve our notch in the world, finding out how hard we could love each other, how hard we could fight. The temper on that woman? Oh, *goddamn,* she was full of fire back then. So full of... life.

But it was great discovering each other, y'know? Everything was new. Exciting. The two of us against the world. We had life by the short and curlies and for a while, we lived life just for ourselves.

Then one day, out of the blue, that all changed.

--==•==--

Her smile is what gives it away.

The alarm clock screams 5:30 in red, angry letters. Some easy listening station snaps on. It's way too damned early to be wailing about heartache, but Elton John is giving it a hell of a try. I slap the snooze button and cut him off in mid-chorus. Maria was never a morning person, so the nine extra minutes in bed is like a gift.

I go through my morning routine. Shower. Shave. Get my suit on and try to thread my five dollar tie. I turn around and Maria's awake, watching me.

Morning sun light streams in between the blinds, and she's washed in bands of gold. The bed sheets are wrapped around her and she's sitting up against the headboard. Her hair is all messed up, but in a good way. Sexy, y'know?

She doesn't say a word. Just gives me this funny little smile full of mischief and hope and this... it's cliché as hell, but this *glow.*

And I knew. I just... *knew.*

That was how I found out I was going to be a father.

--==•==--

When Georgie was born, his face was the color of wet

slate. His umbilical cord was wrapped around his neck. The nurses scrambled to get the doctor some snips and he cut the cord, but Georgie lay there, still and limp as a dishrag. The doctor flipped him over on his stomach and gave him a smack on the ass. I can still remember the wet sound of latex gloves on Georgie's newborn skin.

The doctor mumbled under his breath. *'Come on back, now. Death can't have you yet,'* and lifted his hand for another slap.

A tiny snuffling cough, and Georgie's first cries rang out in the room. The three of us huddled there in the delivery room, tired, laughing, tears flowing down our faces. Just so relieved. Happy.

That's how we became a family.

--==•==--

Upstairs, the noises have stopped. Georgie was excited earlier. Angry. Throwing things. The oak bed thumped against the floor. I heard something shatter and I know I should've boarded the windows. I hope like hell he doesn't break them again.

If I go up there, I know what I'll find – the remnants of a child's tantrum. But I won't see him. He hardly ever shows himself unless he gets *really* upset. He just keeps to the shadows, but he'll never leave me.

Georgie was screaming in his *almost-voice* and even in the middle of his rage, hearing him again almost broke my heart.

He wasn't really speaking though. The noises he makes are primal, closer to the sounds a wounded animal might make. But it's quiet now, as if he's holding his breath, waiting to see what will happen.

--==•==--

Georgie got his looks from Maria. Would've been a real

heart breaker when he got older. Dark hair, olive skin and long lashes framing eyes the color of damp moss. He looked so full of mischief you couldn't help but smile.

Maria was a great mom y'know? You should've seen her and Georgie together, the way they laughed and carried on. Those two were best friends. They meshed. They were... *effortless.*

I used to put him to bed sometimes. Read him a story. Sing to him. We used to do this thing. He'd give me a big hug, plant a tiny, wet kiss on my lips and lay down, teddy bear pulled close, and we'd do our nightly exchange.

Night, night, Georgie.

Night, night, Daddy.

Love you.

Love you too, Daddy.

Who's your buddy?

Me. Who's your pal?

Me.

He'd yawn. His eyelids would smooth and close, flickering as he drifted off. I'd watch him as he lay there at peace. Angelic.

Nothing at all like what he is now.

Being a father changed everything. I started acting the part and got promoted at the company. Me managing employees, believe that? Maria and I bought a place out of the city and for the next few years it was yule logs and egg nog, backyard barbecues and t-ball and all the shit I used to make fun of, y'know? But it was a good life.

It was a *good* life.

Watching Georgie discover things was addicting. His excitement at learning something new. His endless questions.

Why do we call oranges, oranges, but don't call apples, reds?

Why does ice float?

Where do we go when we die?

At get togethers, adults would have conversations with him and walk away shaking their heads, ready to mix themselves a fresh drink. They said Georgie had an old soul.

He was a smart kid, way beyond his years. We'd sidestepped questions about Santa Claus and the Easter Bunny, but Maria and I both knew, at best, we only had a few years before he figured things out.

No question he loved the presents that Christmas brought with it. Watching him run around during an Easter Egg hunt was enough to make you piss yourself laughing.

But Georgie's favorite was Halloween. Cheap plastic masks. Loose fitting polyester costumes. Georgie loved all of it. I think it was the idea of becoming something else for the night that made it so much fun for him. But like any kid, the candy itself was what he loved most. He called it his pirate booty.

We had grilled the rules into him since his first time trick or treating. After we got back home, Maria or I had to check through his candy before he could eat anything. No exceptions.

He was almost five when it happened. Old enough to know better.

--==•==--

The night air is crisp. Downright cold really. Each time the kids yell trick or treat, tiny clouds of steam curl from their mouths. I can almost feel winter bullying its way past fall.

Georgie's ghost costume is stretched tight and shiny over his thin jacket. We've been out for a couple hours already and his cheeks are roses. Georgie's all smiles. His bag is heavy and he's had a pretty good haul for the night. Even so, Maria still has to bribe him with a promise of hot chocolate to steer him back home without an argument.

Just as I open the front door, the phone rings. I hurry

inside, Maria and Georgie behind me. I grab the phone, praying it's not the office calling me tonight, so I'm thankful, but still groan inwardly at a telemarketer reading a script about replacement windows.

I'm tired, but I know the guy's just doing his job. I try to be polite, keep my temper in check, do my best to slip in a *thank-you-but-I'm-not-interested* so I can hang up. I'm still holding the phone as I turn around and watch it all in slow motion.

The apple is a gleaming, polished, beautiful thing. It's oversized in Georgie's tiny hands and a brilliant red against his ghost costume. His mouth opens wide. The bright rectangles of his teeth sink into the burnished skin.

A silver hairline breaks the surface of the apple but I notice it far too late.

Georgie bites in deep and so does the razor blade inside. Blood gushes from his mouth, paints the front of his costume with a red exclamation point.

The apple tumbles from his hands and falls to the carpet. It leaves a bloody trail as it rolls to a stop at my feet. Georgie looks at me, confused. He knows something's wrong, but the pain hasn't hit yet.

Georgie puts his hands to his mouth and withdraws something pink and spongy. He waves it at me and begins jumping up and down, making this high pitched mewling. His expression turns to panic.

I run to him. I scream for Maria to call 9-1-1.

Georgie tries to talk and it comes out a garbled mess. He coughs, makes this liquid, whistling sound from the back of his throat. He claws at his neck. More blood streams from his mouth and he falls to his knees, choking. I turn him over and cradle him in my lap, try to work inside his mouth. My hands grow slick. The razor slices into the tips of my fingers, and my blood mingles with my son's. The blade's there, wedged at the back of his throat, but I can't get it free.

Georgie convulses on my lap and as little as he is, it's all I can do to hold him still. The world around me grows quiet.

I know Maria's beside me. I can see her screaming but I can't hear her. Red spirals of light twist over my living room walls. I know the paramedics are out front but I don't hear sirens.

I know they're too late.

Georgie's expression pleads with me to fix this, to put it all back together again because I'm the guy who does that. I'm the dryer of crocodile tears and the healer of boo-boos. I'm the slayer of bedtime monsters and the mechanic of broken toys.

I'm... I'm *Daddy*.

But Daddy can't fix this.

All the king's horses and all the king's men can't *fix this*.

Georgie's legs stop shaking. More blood pours from his mouth, black as oil. His body stops trembling, gets rigid. His gaze is still locked on mine.

I don't know what I expected to see in his eyes, but I didn't think it would be the anger I found. The rage.

Georgie's eyes begin to lose their shine. His small chest stops moving and his body relaxes. I feel him lift up and pass through me; a sensation like a cold breeze against sunburned skin.

Sound kicks in again. I hear the heavy footsteps of the paramedics as they run into the house. Strong hands pull Georgie away from me. They lead Maria from the room. The paramedics work on his body but it's useless. He's already gone.

And I can't stop screaming.

--==•==--

Two months passed before Georgie came back.

Maria and I had become little more than roomates, both of us lost in a sea of grief, unable to get to shore. She couldn't comfort me and I couldn't comfort her and to be perfectly honest, I don't think either one of us cared anymore. Something inside us died along with our son. We were both numb, drifting off into memories of when he was alive, so it took us a while to realize that Georgie was dead, but he wasn't gone.

It was little things at first. Cold pockets of air traveled around the house. Matchbox cars rolled across the hardwood floor of his bedroom. In the middle of the night, the television would flick on, blaring cartoons. I'd be standing in the kitchen and feel small, icy hands tugging at the back of my leg.

Georgie kept getting stronger.

We woke in the middle of the night to find him standing at the foot of our bed. Georgie stared at me with his angry face and milky eyes, hate streaming off him in waves. His mouth opened in a yawn and blood spilled free. Georgie pointed a single accusing finger at me. His breath carried the fetid smell of old blood and rotted apples. Then he faded into the shadows.

Maria left that night. Didn't look at me, didn't cry, just drove off. Hell, she never even came back for her goddamn clothes, just set her wedding ring on the counter, grabbed her keys and ran. Our attorneys took care of everything else. Last I heard, she moved to Seattle and started nursing school. Married an engineer I think, maybe an accountant, I can't remember. Sounds like a quiet life, though. Safe. *Predictable.*

I'm happy for Maria. Really, I am. I can't blame her. Georgie's anger lies with me, not her.

But after she left, I was alone with him.

I started sleeping with the lights on, but I could still see Georgie moving in the shadows. I tried shutting the bedroom door but could still hear him scratching, the door knob rattling, as he whispered from the hallway.

"Night, night Daddeeeeeeeeee."

Even now, sometimes I'll wake from sleep, the feeling of tiny, cold hands against my throat, choking off my air. Rows of bloody scratches cover my arms. Crescents of bite marks pattern my legs.

It's a horrible thing to be afraid of your own child. I'd be lying if I said that ending it all hasn't crossed my mind.

Some days I think it would be so easy to sit in a hot bath and put a razor to my wrist. Just watch my life spool away in red ribbons.

It's ironic, really. What drove Maria away is the same thing keeping me here. Fear is its own prison and it doesn't need bars.

See, I can't help but wonder, if Georgie is this angry with me now…if he torments me this much while I'm still alive… what's he going to do to me when I'm dead?

--==•==--

I know why Georgie's angry. He's lonely.

Sometimes the loneliness gets to me but mostly I've learned to live with it. But Georgie...his pain I can't bear anymore.

I can hear the children outside, their excited squeals as they walk from door to door. Flashlight beams dance through the streets and I know any second I'll hear footsteps on the porch and the kids will ring my doorbell. Their painted faces will be full of smiles as they hold out their bags, waiting for the promise of candy.

This year, I've made...*special* treats for the kids.

Georgie wants a playmate and I intend to give him one.

Georgie's angry. He's lonely.

But I can fix this. I'm the guy who does that.

I'm the dryer of crocodile tears and the healer of boo-boos. I'm the slayer of bedtime monsters and the mechanic of broken toys.

I'm Daddy.

END

AUTHOR'S NOTES

RACING THE MILK

Every writer worth their salt knows the phrase "bleeding on the page". I'm very guilty of utilizing this method, turning every bit of emotional turmoil and pain into writing fodder. Though it may be wrapped in metaphors, most who know me very well can pick out the kernels of truth and the origin of what the story came from. Racing the Milk was written and rewritten during a time in my life when things were leading to a divorce in my life. Dark days, indeed. Fighting through those times and writing feelings down were my method of trying to get it out of me. Exorcising demons, so to speak. Sometimes it helps, sometimes you just remain haunted, but I figured it was worth a try.

This story absolutely destroys the audience when I do live readings. I once had a woman in the crowd who was completely sobbing, trying to keep quiet. After, she came up and called me an asshole for ruining her make-up, then gave me a hug. One of the best compliments I've ever gotten as a writer.

EARLY HARVEST

I don't even remember the inspiration for this one, but it appeared in Lamplight magazine and I was the highlighted author that issue. I've always been intrigued by the underbelly of society. The hookers, bartenders, the garbage truck men. The every day people we don't seem to notice very often. The people we rely on day in and day out, but don't really pay that much attention to. People from the backwoods regions, away from the American Dream neighborhoods are no exception. I opted on the pen pal delivery one morning and it went from there. The image of looking down a dark well and seeing a pale hand reaching out into the sunlight had been with me for a while and I had no idea what it meant. Things collided one late night along with a bit of tequila, and Early Harvest is the result.

BLUEBOTTLE SUMMER

This story was born out of fear and it's all Brian Keene's fault. Not very long after meeting Keene for the first time, he invited me to a cook out at his house. In his email, he told me there would be late night readings, and I had BETTER bring something to read.

Understand, I had been building my ad business and focusing on that instead of pursuing my real passion of writing and there was really nothing I had suitable for reading. I wrote Bluebottle Summer over two days and brought it with me to the cookout. True to his word, when the party began dying down, we were all gathered around and readings began. Even Geoff Cooper read (and witnessing him not READ a story, but TELL a story... absolutely becoming the character in his story Turning Leaves... that is a memory I will never forget and set me on a path of learning the best methods of doing live readings). A few days after the cookout, Brian called me. I'd left my manuscript pages behind and his (now) ex-wife had picked it up and read it. She mentioned to Brian that it was one hell of a story and Brian's response was "Who knew the fucker could write!"

THE TASTE OF OUR INDISCRETIONS

Some great writers in the field, Maurice Broaddus and Jerry Gordon, put together a celebrated anthology called Dark Faith. They had some great submissions and created a companion chapbook for the release called Last Rites. This story appeared in the chapbook and has become increasingly difficult to find. Joseph Haslan, the main character learns you reap what you sow in life.

FOR GOODNESS SAKE

A happy little holiday tale. I have notes set aside for a project called Tales to Make Children Cry at Night, and I guess this was a test in that arena. I'm an only child and never had to deal with siblings and I thought having a psycho in childhood dealing with Santa Claus and getting jealous might be a fun thing to play with.

BABY'S BREATH

When I lived in Philadelphia for a couple of years, two of my best friends worked at a video store. The store manager was quite a character and when he left for another job, he left behind a scrapbook of newspaper clippings ranging from articles on Natalie Wood, Stephen King, John Travolta and the opening night of Pink Floyd's The Wall at a theater in Philadelphia. I adopted the scrapbook and took it on my own to start adding to it. For the longest time I started clipping out odd or gruesome articles from the morning paper. The first mention of cannibal atrocities in Milwaukee (an unnamed Jeffrey Dahmer), and assorted other articles of some really bad shit happening around the world. I kept that up for a long time until it became tiring and disheartening to actually read the daily news because it seemed like there were so many bad things happening. One of the articles entailed a newborn infant being abducted from a hospital and that was the inspiration for the flash piece I wrote.

IN COUNTRY

Lamplight is a magazine run by my good friend and very talented Jacob Haddon. His magazine and the releases from Apokrupha Publishing are all top notch and well thought out. He's doing it right, where so many others just don't seem to be able to think it through clearly before launching into a magazine or publishing house. In Country was a short tale blended from the stories I've heard from war veterans and the massage parlors scattered throughout Philadelphia.

IN DARKER WATERS
There's an anthology out titled Fell Beasts, edited by Ty Schwamberger centering around beast stories. In Darker Waters found a home among its pages. As a young kid, I grew up around ponds and lakes and streams and never once stopped to think about what lay beneath the murky waters as I went swimming in them. It's strange, I think, the older I became, the more that fear got to me, and I cannot even recall the last time I swam in waters where I couldn't at least see a foot or so down. What can I say? Not knowing what lies beneath creeps me the fuck out.

FREE RIDE ANGIE
I'm an odd writer in that I get titles all the time. Little snips of this or that come to me and I've learned to jot them down and let the story attached to it come to me. Free Ride Angie is no exception. The title came to me on a drive back from my honeymoon, driving a long stretch of I-95 headed back north. All I had was the title and that it was about a prostitute who exchanged sex for free cab rides.

Wasn't until about three years later when it all clicked into place and when I sat down to write the story, it seemed less like writing and more like dictating Angie's character in my head. She was the first time I experienced a voice so strong that when I had finished writing, I looked over bits and pieces of the dialogue and was taken back because there were some phrases and terms I personally would never use. She became absolutely alive to me.

And that, my friends, is magic. There's nothing else like it.

BREEDING SEASON
This was a little flash piece I submitted online for Alien Candle Shop.

BLOODLEGUM & LOLLIKNIVES
I have an amazing son and daughter and I love them both dearly. They're smart and hilarious and get their twisted sense of humor from me. When they were young, we were all out trick or treating one year and my son, about three years old at the time, came walking back from a house with his goody bag raised high. I asked him what he got and his toddler language replied "Bloodlegum" which, translated into bubblegum.

The term stuck in my mind (no pun intended).

Time moved on and as it got close to Christmas that year, Brian Keene was developing a give-away for his fans on his online message forum as a thank you. Myself and several other great writers were in a chapbook called New Dawn — another complete rarity to find these days — and his fans really liked the gift. I most often get fans who mention the puppy scene in this story. Makes me giggle every time.

MAGGIE BLUE
I worked at an ad agency for a while, years ago, and not long after I started working there, the offices moved from the third floor to a larger office space in the basement of the building. It was expansive, perfect for adding new staff members and stretching out a bit. But it also had the lovely attraction of cockroaches from time to time. One of my co-workers, a lovely girl by the name of Amber Topper, was deathly afraid of bugs of any kind. There was a dead roach on the floor one day and I saw her climb over her desk and scale a bookshelf faster than a starving spider monkey after fresh fruit. I decided to write

a story that would be completely and utterly disgusting and embrace that fear. For the record, those damned "eyebrow bugs" that pop up sometimes in the house? The ones that look like Magnum PI's mustache ran off his face and is crawling on the walls? Yeah, those. I'll scream like a schoolgirl over those damned things. Hate 'em. I'd rather set the house on fire and just move.

OF ALL EVIL

JF Gonzalez was one of the first writers I met and because I was still pretty new at all of it, I was following everyone's lead. I no longer remember where this story got published, but I know it was an online venue that paid mid-rates. I had seen a short that Gonzalez had published on the site and I followed suit and submitted Of All Evil. Sure enough, I got paid but I think this was probably my second sale ever. You can definitely tell this is an early work from me but here it is, warts and all. Take it for what you will. I think at the time, I was probably working close to 70 hours a week running my ad agency, and really felt cornered into the situation of not having any choice but to keep doing what I was doing. I was feeling pretty damned run down and getting disgusted with the greed of the ad field.

PLEASING MARLENA

This story and my novel The Compound, are the only pieces of zombie fiction I've ever done. I often get asked about this piece, "What's with the Ashton Kutcher hate?"

I don't really hate Ashton, but everyone on the planet knew who he was after he started dating Demi Moore and he seemed like a good target for the story. This was picked up on a World War Z web site (before the movie came out), and fans seemed to dig the tale. My fiction is almost always based on the characters and this one is no exception. It's a man caring for his wife in her dying days. The zombie apocalypse just happens to be going on at the same time.

GEORGIE

Ahhhhh Georgie.

Remember me talking about bleeding on the page? Georgie a prime example. I never explained this publicly to anyone until recently at a convention after doing a live reading of it. Yes, the story, on the outside, is about a Father's love/fear for his son. But the core of it... the truth is, this story is based on a man haunted by his inability to save his marriage. He's haunted and agonized by himself and his inabilities. No matter what he does or where he goes, the ghosts still go with him. Wrap that personal anguish in some metaphors and tie it together with the urban tales of psychos putting razor blades into Halloween treats and this is what you arrive at. It appeared in an absolutely amazing Halloween issue of Shroud magazine, edited by the incredibly talented Kevin Lucia.

**Additional note... this happens to be one of my favorite stories to read to a live audience, if for nothing else, I made Brian Keene cry. Usually every father in the audience is doomed when they hear this one read out loud. And that kind of emotional impact is what I strive for.*

AFTERWORD

So there you have it, my fine friends. I can't possibly thank you enough for reading my tales. As always, there's a lot of insanity going on in my life, but I'm really trying to be more prolific in creating new work — both for you, as well as me.

Thank you from the bottom of my heart for every sentence of mine you read, for every compliment or review you post, for every laugh or tear you've had through reading one of my stories. You are all so greatly, greatly appreciated, I'll never be able to explain it.

But I promise I'll try.

Bob Ford
July 4, 2014

Manchester, PA

Robert Ford fills his days running an ad agency and considering ripping the phone lines from the wall. He has published various short fiction and has several screenplays floating around in the ether of Hollywood. He can confirm the grass actually is greener on the other side, but it's only because of the bodies buried there. Visit coronersreport.blogspot.com to find out what he's currently working on, or if his committal papers to the asylum have been processed.

Long fiction by Robert Ford:
(available in Kindle and print)

The Compound

Samson and Denial

Made in the USA
Middletown, DE
19 February 2019